The first day of school

It was like that dream where you go to school naked, only worse, because it was real. I spotted the band of elastic sticking out from the bottom of my pant leg. I yanked it free, and Mom's panties billowed forth in a blossom of shiny nylon. As if they were mine. As if they'd slipped off my body and down my leg, which was utterly impossible, but did anybody care?

"Strip show, baby!" called Jeremy Webster. "Take it *all* off!" Another guy whistled, and others hooted and clapped.

At me and my mother's underwear, exposed to the world in all our freaking glory.

OTHER BOOKS YOU MAY ENJOY

Agnes Parker: Girl in Progress — Kathleen O'Dell

Dizzy — Cathy Cassidy

Eleven — Lauren Myracle

The English Roses: Friends for Life — Madonna

The English Roses: Good-bye, Grace? — Madonna

The English Roses: The New Girl — Madonna

The English Roses: A Rose by Any Other Name — Madonna

How My Private, Personal Journal Became a Bestseller — Julia DeVillers

Indigo Blue — Cathy Cassidy

Notes from a Liar and Her Dog — Gennifer Choldenko

Olivia Kidney — Ellen Potter

Ophie Out of Oz — Kathleen O'Dell

The Red Rose Box — Brenda Woods

Twelve — Lauren Myracle

LAUREN MYRACLE

the fashion disaster that changed my life

PUFFIN BOOKS

PUFFIN BOOKS
Published by the Penguin Group
Penguin Young Readers Group, 345 Hudson Street, New York, New York 10014, U.S.A.
Penguin Group (Canada), 90 Eglinton Avenue, Suite 700, Toronto, Ontario, Canada M4P 2Y3
(a division of Pearson Penguin Canada Inc.)
Penguin Books Ltd, 80 Strand, London WC2R 0RL, England
Penguin Ireland, 25 St Stephen's Green, Dublin 2, Ireland (a division of Penguin Books Ltd)
Penguin Group (Australia), 250 Camberwell Road, Camberwell, Victoria 3124, Australia
(a division of Pearson Australia Group Pty Ltd)
Penguin Books India Pvt Ltd, 11 Community Centre, Panchsheel Park, New Delhi - 110 017, India
Penguin Group (NZ), 67 Apollo Drive, Rosedale, North Shore 0632, New Zealand
(a division of Pearson New Zealand Ltd)
Penguin Books (South Africa) (Pty) Ltd, 24 Sturdee Avenue, Rosebank, Johannesburg 2196, South Africa

Registered Offices: Penguin Books Ltd, 80 Strand, London WC2R 0RL, England

First published in the United States of America by Dutton Children's Books,
a division of Penguin Young Readers Group, 2005
Published by Puffin Books, a division of Penguin Young Readers Group, 2007

1 3 5 7 9 10 8 6 4 2

CIP Data is available.

Puffin Books ISBN 978-0-14-240717-2

Designed by Irene Vandervoort

Printed in the United States of America

For Mom, the fashion queen

Acknowledgments

Thanks to Jack Martin, Laura Pritchett, Catherine Larkins, and Ruth White for giving such good advice along the way. Thanks to Amber Kelley for helping me carve out time to write. Thanks to Sarah Shumway for her able assistance. And a big hug for Julie Strauss-Gabel, who helped me uncover the story that was meant to be. (I'd give you a kitten if I could!)

the **fashion disaster**
that **changed my life**

Tuesday, September 5, 3:25 P.M.

Why does everything in my life have to go so wrong?! Why?!!
Out of all the people in the world, why do I have to be the freak
who went to school on the very first day of the year with a pair
of PANTIES stuck by static cling to the leg of my pants?!!!

*La, la, la, isn't life great—WHOOPS! Oh dear, would you
look at that? It's Mom's underwear, popping out to say a big
hello!!!*

And now I can't stop crying, which only makes me feel more
pathetic. But really, it's so incredibly unfair. I mean, this was
going to be my breakout year. The year I finally stopped being
invisible.

I stopped being invisible, all right.

I had planned on wearing jeans. Nice, normal jeans with a sprinkling of tiny rhinestones, like raindrops, along the outlines of the front pockets. But could I? *Noooo,* because they were still in the wash—thanks, Mom—which meant I had to root through the dryer for my gray drawstring pants instead. And then I had to dash back upstairs and change shirts, because while my "Pebbles" T-shirt looked good with jeans, it looked really stupid with the gray drawstrings.

By the time I got to homeroom, everyone was already seated. I hurried to Ms. Larson's desk to collect our back-to-school handouts, and that's when I heard someone snicker, then someone else, and someone else. Before long, everyone in the class was rolling with laughter.

I got a stomach-dropping feeling. "What's so funny?" I asked.

"Your panties, man!" Jeremy Webster howled. "You're losing your panties!"

I looked down, but saw nothing. I craned my neck to look behind me.

"There!" said Samantha Greene, pointing at my pant leg.

Time stopped.

It was like that dream where you go to school naked, only worse, because it was real. I spotted the band of elastic sticking out from the bottom of my pant leg. I yanked it free, and Mom's panties billowed forth in a blossom of shiny nylon. As if they were mine. As if they'd slipped off my body and down my leg, which was utterly impossible, but did anybody care?

"Strip show, baby!" called Jeremy Webster. "Take it *all* off!" Another guy whistled, and others hooted and clapped.

At me and my mother's underwear, exposed to the world in all our freaking glory.

Same day, 3:52 P.M.

Just got off the phone with Kathy, who somehow managed to make me feel worse than I already did. And if I don't write it down, the whole conversation will just keep bouncing around in my head. Writing stuff down doesn't always help, but at least I can read back over it and say, "Oh. Yes. You're completely right to be so depressed."

So here it is, the instant replay of my shame, according to Kathy:

Kathy: "Omigod, Alli. What happened to you today? Jeremy Webster's been telling everyone that you did a striptease during homeroom, that you whipped off your underwear in front of the whole class and—"

Me: "Kathy!"

Kathy: "He's calling you the *stripper of the seventh grade,* Alli. Now tell me what happened!!!"

Me: "A pair of underwear happened to be stuck inside my pant leg. It was static cling. And I did not do a striptease. I just pulled them out of my pants and shoved them in my backpack, okay?"

Kathy: "Omigod."

Me: "And they weren't mine. They were my mom's."

Kathy: "Omigod. Alli, that is the most embarrassing thing I've ever heard."

Me: "Yeah, well, thanks."

Kathy: "I'm so serious. I mean, geez, you had your mom's big old nasty underwear dangling from your—"

Me: "Yes, Kathy. I was there, remember? Anyway, I've got to go."

Kathy: "Fine, whatever. I'll see you tomorrow. But Alli?"

Me: "What?"

Kathy: "I'm only saying this for your own good, but be sure to check your clothes before you leave. I mean, next time it could be a bra, or one of your dad's *jockstraps*, and—"

Me: (hanging up the phone) *Click.*

Kathy's my best friend, but she doesn't know very much about cheering me up. Lately I've been thinking that she doesn't know much about me, period. But then I feel bad, because even if Kathy's not as perfect as I want her to be, she's gone out of her way to be there for me. Ever since last year, when being popular suddenly became important. When Rachel Delaney became queen, and I disappeared.

Kathy stuck by me then, and I know she'll stick by me now. Like glue.

Wednesday, September 6, 7:37 A.M.

I set my alarm for six-thirty to make sure I'd have plenty of time to get ready this morning. Then I threw half my clothes on the floor, including a horrible burgundy jumper and my too-small cargo pants, before settling on a white T-shirt and a tan miniskirt. Nothing clinging to either. I checked.

"Good morning, Allison," Mom said when I came down for breakfast. "Are you doing better today?"

I clamped my lips together. I knew I wasn't being fair, but I couldn't help feeling that if she had folded the laundry like a good mother, none of this would have happened.

"Could I have a napkin, please?" I asked. I used it to wrap up my Pop-Tart, which I brought back up here to eat. To my room, where no one can ask me pointless questions like, "Are you doing better today?"

Because today is not about doing "better." "Better" isn't good enough. Today is about putting my old life completely behind me and starting fresh, which was my goal for this school year all along. Only inside, I don't feel like a brand-new me at all. I feel like the same old dorky me who missed two months of school last year—through no fault of my own—and turned into a social nobody. The same dorky me who memorized the opening sequence of *The Young and the Restless* and who chubbed out from lying in Mom's bed day after day. Kathy claimed I got a spare tire. She also claimed I was faking, that I was never really sick at all.

But why would I have done that? At the beginning of sixth grade, I was friends with everybody, not just Kathy. *Everybody* was friends with everybody. But by second semester of that same year, when I came back after being absent for so long, the girls carried Tampax in their purses and giggled if someone didn't wear deodorant. All the rules had changed, and I no longer knew how to play the game.

I was no longer *in* the game.

Same day, social studies

I am writing furiously while Mr. Shakley lectures us on the British colonization of America, which I've learned about every year since second grade. But I'm frowning and pretending to take notes, because Jeremy Webster is leering at me from three desks over, and I refuse to meet his gaze. I will not look up. I will not look up. I WILL NOT LOOK UP.

This morning in homeroom, Jeremy blocked my path and pretended to do a striptease, wiggling his hips and crooning, "Da-da-da-*boom*, da-da-*boom*, da-da-*boom*."

My heart got all fast in my chest. "Please move," I whispered.

"Ooo, baby, I *AM* moving," he said. He bumped me with his hip. "Hey, why don't you get a job at the Pussycat Palace? Then you could get paid to take off your undies."

I know I turned bright red, because I could feel it. I pushed past him, and he said, "Ow! This pussycat has claws!"

Mika Satomi saw it all, which made it even worse. Jeremy would never pick on Mika. He wouldn't dare. Because Mika is second-in-command to Rachel Delaney, and everyone knows that Rachel rules the school.

"He's a jerk," Mika said as I slid into my chair. "Don't let him get to you."

I shrugged. I was in that trembly stage of trying not to cry.

She studied me with her dark eyes. Then the bell rang, and she jumped up and hurried into the hall. "Rachel! Hadley!" I heard her call. "Wait up!"

And now here I am, stuck in fourth-period social studies with not only Jeremy and Mika but Hadley and Rachel, too. It's so so wrong. Rachel is doodling in her notebook, tilting it every so often toward Hadley, who covers her mouth to hide her smile. She's wearing silver earrings shaped like butterflies. Rachel, not Hadley. Her brown hair is so glossy it gleams, and she holds her spine like she's afraid of no one.

Last spring Rachel invented a game called "Kiss the Boy," where she and Mika and Hadley would chase a boy around the playground and blitz him with kisses. Kathy scoffed and said how dumb it was, how tacky, but I watched and wished I were that brave.

They never chased Jeremy, though. With his greasy hair and show-offy voice, Jeremy is actually lower on the totem pole than I am, which makes his stripper jokes even more humiliating. And now here we all are in Mr. Shakley's social studies class, one big happy family.

Thursday, September 7, 4:45 P.M.

I just logged off the computer after IM-ing with Kathy, who's planning a sleepover for Saturday night. She's inviting me and Megan Campbell, who's new this year. Megan used to live in Colorado, and she doesn't wear any makeup, which is unusual for our grade. But she's got great hair, short and blond and messy in a really cute way. In fact, the three of us together would make a terrific hair ad: Kathy with her spazzy red curls, Megan with her short blond tufts, and me with my straight brown hair. Kathy says we should call ourselves the Hair Sisters.

But my hair, like everything else about me, is going through a difficult stage these days. I read an article in Mom's *Cosmo* that said to stop washing your hair for a week and it'll turn "phenomenally lustrous and soft." You're not supposed to panic when it starts to get greasy, because on the fifth or sixth day, it'll go around the bend and look clean again.

On the other hand, perhaps this is not the time for experiments.

At any rate, I'm glad Megan's joining us on Saturday, because sometimes it feels like a lot, just me and Kathy all the time. As we were finishing IM-ing, Kathy informed me that she told her sister about my "accident." My muscles tightened when I read that, because Leslie is in the tenth grade, and she's always telling Kathy and me how dumb we are. "I was, too, when I was your age," Leslie says. "And then I started high school, and I was like, 'Oh. *Now* I get it.'"

Anyway, I'm going to paste in the part that came next:

MizKitty: ur not mad, r u?
allisongrace: what did leslie say?
MizKitty: oh, she thought it was really sad.
allisongrace: she laffed, didn't she?
MizKitty: well . . . just at first. but then she said it was really sad.

I felt bad deep down inside when I read that. I wanted to say something to Kathy, like, "Please don't tell anyone else," but I knew if I did, it would make things even worse.

Same night, 8:22 P.M.

I think Kathy knows she screwed up, because she just sent me an e-card. It said, "A special present just for you. Click here to open jar." I clicked on the lid of the jar, and all these balls of fluff with happy faces came out and started floating around the screen. They looked kind of like mutant sheep. The message at the bottom of the screen read, "Here are some warm fuzzies to make your day brighter."

Saturday, September 9, 3:45 P.M.

I'm off to Kathy's as soon as Mom finishes grading her stack of essays. At breakfast I apologized for being a pain the last couple of days, and Dad put down his toast and said, "You mean because of the great underwear fiasco?"

I gripped my fork and wished I'd kept quiet. I hate it when he turns something real into something to joke about.

"I'm teasing. I'm teasing," he said. He held up his thumb and forefinger as if measuring off an inch. "But you've got to admit, it was just a tiny bit——"

"Dan," Mom interrupted. "Let her finish."

I nudged my eggs. "Well, that's all I wanted to say. That I'm sorry."

Mom came over and gave me a hug. "Thanks, Allison. I'm sorry, too."

Kathy, Megan, and I went to the mall, where we pawed through the sales rack at Express and checked out the earrings at Claire's. Now we're back at Kathy's, and Kathy and Megan are watching *Nick at Nite*. I'm half watching and half writing, because a lot happened that I want to think about. Like how we were eating waffle fries at the food court, and out of nowhere Kathy said to Megan, "Alli used to be fat. Can you believe it?"

Megan looked at me. I blushed.

"No way," she said. "You're, like, tiny."

"*Now* she is," Kathy said. "But last year she had this mysterious illness and missed four months of school. If she had missed any more, she was going to be held back."

"For real?" Megan asked.

"Two months," I said. "I only missed two months." Kathy doesn't get how awful that whole time was for me, how I do not like talking about it at all.

"Wow," Megan said. "So . . . what was wrong? Are you better now?"

She seemed really worried, so Kathy jumped in and said, "It wasn't cancer or anything like that. It was an ear infection; that's what they finally figured out." She dipped a fry into a blob of ketchup. "My mom was like, 'If my children stayed home for four months every time they had an ear infection . . .'"

"*Two* months," I said.

"Anyway, she really porked out. It was hysterical."

Megan looked uncomfortable. "I'm sure you didn't pork out," she said to me.

"Are you kidding?" Kathy said. "She watched soap operas and ate Doritos all day." She laughed, but no one joined in. Her smile grew less sure. "I mean, you look terrific now. Obviously."

"I got dizzy whenever I tried to stand," I explained to Megan. "So I kind of had to stay in bed all the time."

"But you got better?" Megan asked. She was being *too* concerned, and I wanted the conversation to be over. I hate that part, when people get all weirded out.

"They gave me megadoses of antibiotics, and I totally went back to normal," I said.

"Well, yeah," Kathy said. "That was my whole point."

She spotted Jared MacIlwaine, and she waved at him maniacally until he bounded over in his I LIVE TO ANNOY T-shirt and gave us some Gummi Worms from the Candy Connection. I was glad for the distraction. After he left, the three of us started talking about guys, and Kathy asked Megan if there was anyone in our grade she had a crush on.

"Nah, not yet," Megan said. She turned to me. "What about you?"

I thought of Aaron Sarmiento with his smiley face and quick laugh. Aaron's in my math class and my social studies class (the only good thing about fourth period), and yesterday he helped me find Cumberland Island on my map of Georgia. I almost told Megan this, but Kathy was already making smooching sounds and trilling, "Jeremy Webster!"

I shoved her. "That is so not true."

"But *he* has a crush on *you*," Kathy said. "Otherwise he wouldn't be picking on you so much."

Megan's eyebrows scrunched together.

"Every day this week he's meowed at me and asked me what color underwear I was wearing," I said. I hitched my shoulders. "It's getting old."

"So tell him to quit," Megan said.

"I *do*. But it doesn't make any difference. Jeremy is . . . I don't know. He's not like other people."

"His brother's in Leslie's grade, and Leslie says he's a freak, too," Kathy said. She dropped her last Gummi Worm into her mouth. "They live in a trailer park with their dad, only their dad's hardly ever there. He works in that truck stop called the Ever Open, and Leslie says that Jeremy and Steve are left to themselves practically all the time."

"Oh, that's sad," Megan said.

Kathy nodded, like, *Yes, isn't it terrible?*

"Still," Megan said, "he shouldn't be mean to you, Alli."

I liked her for saying that, because it was like she was standing up for me, sort of.

She actually just stood up for me again, right here in Kathy's basement. I guess I've been writing for too long, because while I was still getting the mall stuff down, Kathy started teasing me about my journal. I could tell she was embarrassed that I was scribbling away during *Bewitched*.

"God, you are so *strange!*" Kathy said for Megan's benefit. She turned to Megan directly. "She has to put everything in her journal. She's obsessed."

"Huh?" Megan said.

"She even glues in e-mails and IMs. It's like nothing ever dies."

"Yeah?" Megan said. "That's cool. Because otherwise they'd just get deleted, wouldn't they? Which when you think about it is kind of sad."

"Nuh-uh," Kathy said. "You could save them on your computer."

"But not forever," Megan said. "And even if you *did* save them on your computer, it's not like you'd ever look at them again. At least, I never do."

Kathy peered at her, trying to decide if she had a point. Uh-oh. Now Kathy's scooting closer and leaning over my shoulder. Great, she's trying to grab the

HAHAHAHAHA! I'm in Alli's journal! I'm famous! And you know you love me, Alli, so quit huffing and puffing. Anyway, you are being very boring, so I am stealing your pen so that you have to pay attention to ME. (Okay, fine. I suppose you can pay attention to Megan, too, just as long as you like me best. JK. Aren't I hilarious?)

Mwah!

Same night, still at Kathy's

I've made a tent out of my sleeping bag, and I'm using Kathy's Sailor Moon flashlight to see the paper. I'm pretty sure Megan's asleep now, because her breathing's gotten slow and regular. And Kathy's been asleep for about an hour. She's doing her *puh-puh-puh* thing, where instead of snoring, she breathes out in little puffs like a steam engine. Megan and I got all giggly about it earlier, only we had to smother ourselves so we wouldn't wake Kathy, which made it even funnier.

After we calmed down, the two of us shifted around on the floor and talked for a while. It was nice, because it felt . . . I don't know. *Real*. Like, Megan told me about Boulder, where she used to live. She misses it, especially now that school's started. She said the guys at her old school weren't as immature as the guys at Sweetwater. There wasn't so much bra-strap popping, and if a guy and a girl got assigned to be partners or something, no one made a big deal out of it.

As we talked, we could hear cars going by outside Kathy's house. I'm used to it, but Megan said, "Kathy sure lives on a busy street, huh? In Boulder, it was never this loud at night." Then she grimaced and said, "You must be so sick of me, going on and on about Colorado."

"I don't mind," I said. "The only place I've ever lived is Atlanta, so I like hearing about other places." I traced the seam of my sleeping bag. "So . . . why did you move? Did your dad get transferred or something?"

Megan hesitated, then said, "My parents got divorced."

"Oh," I said.

"And now my mom hates my dad so much that she couldn't even stay in the same state with him, so she applied for a job here. And she got it, so we moved."

I wished I hadn't asked. "Oh."

"You know what the worst thing is?"

"Um . . . what?"

She didn't answer, and I didn't know what to do. Should I

just wait? But for how long? I didn't want her to think I didn't care.

"I had to leave my cat behind," she said at last. "Because our new apartment doesn't allow pets."

I could hear how sad she was, and I held myself still. I wanted to touch her arm or something, but I didn't know how. "What was her name?"

"Fred. He's a boy. We gave him to our next-door neighbors. They already had three cats, and they were like, 'Sure, whatever.' But I know Mrs. Fitzhugh's not going to give him the right food. He needs Science Diet, but they feed their cats Happy Cat out of a can, which is really bad because it's got intestines and toenails and things like that in it."

"Ick."

"I know. I hate my mom for making us leave him behind. And I hate my dad for making us leave in the first place."

"You mean because he wanted a divorce?"

She made this laughing sound, only not really. "Because he fell in love with his secretary and moved into her condo. Isn't that pathetic?"

I pressed my cheek into the smoothness of my pillow. I didn't know what to say. "Megan—"

"I know. It's okay."

"No, it's not. It's awful."

Megan rolled away from me and said, "Honest to God, Alli, I miss Fred more than I miss my dad." She was silent for a few moments. Then she said, "Don't tell, okay?" Megan asked. "Any of it."

"I won't," I said.

And now Megan's asleep, but not me, because my brain won't stop thinking about it all. About how Dad would never do that, fall in love with someone else and leave me and Mom to start a whole new life. And about how glad I am—although I'd never say that to Megan.

I think it's so amazing that she told me in the first place. I don't know how people do that, just open themselves up and let what's inside of them come out. When she was telling me, *I* got all nervous, and it wasn't even me doing the talking.

I wanted to, kind of. Talk, that is. Like about last year, maybe, and how I know what it's like to be lonely. How the teachers were so nice when I finally came back to school, and how that actually made things worse. Like that day Mrs. Pearce put her arm around me during recess and walked me over to Hadley, who was taking a quick break from "Kiss the Boy" to get a rock out of her sandal.

"Hadley, this is Alli," Mrs. Pearce said, as if I was new.

Hadley gave me a look. "Yeah, I know," she said.

Mrs. Pearce gave me a squeeze, then released me. "Well, I know you girls want to get on with your game. You don't need an old duck like me hanging around!"

She left, and Hadley succeeded in fishing out the rock. She ran off to Rachel without a backward glance. I stood there, blushing, until Kathy came and got me and led me to the steps. Kathy complained about how shallow Hadley was—how shallow Rachel's whole clique was—although even then I knew it was because she, like me, wasn't one of them.

Oh my God, that sounds horrible. Kathy was really nice to me when no one else was. She passed notes to me and ate lunch with me and called me after school, every single day without fail. Only, sometimes she acted as if she owned me. Like, she'd make a point of bringing up my spare tire when other people were around, almost as if she wanted to make me look bad on purpose. So that no one else would want me, I guess. But she'd do it in a teasing way to show that she *did* want me. That I was hers.

And even though we're in seventh grade now—which really is so different from sixth—sometimes it feels like she's doing the same thing.

Maybe I would have talked to Megan about it, if she'd been awake. And I'd have told her that I didn't used to be fat. Just chubby.

But probably not.

Sunday, September 10, Neiman Marcus makeup counter

Mom is dabbing at herself with eye creams, and I am perched on a stool trying to ignore the makeup lady with the big hair. Inside, I am dying. Not because of the makeup lady, but because of Rachel Delaney, who we ran into at the chichi restaurant where Mom and I just ate lunch. Rachel is someone I have to gear up for, even at school when I know to expect her. To be face-to-face with her unexpectedly is totally unfair.

"Alli!" Rachel cried when she spotted me. She and her parents were leaving as Mom and I walked in. She was wearing a funky red dress with a silver dragon on it, and she had on actual heels. "Look how cute you are!"

I felt a sinking sensation. I don't think Rachel was trying to be mean, but suddenly my yellow sundress seemed totally wrong. Compared to her, I looked like a kindergartner.

"Hi, Rachel," I said.

She stepped closer. "So we did it, huh?" She slapped me a high five, which I wasn't prepared for. "We survived the first week of school!"

"Um, yeah." I tried to smile.

I must not have been very convincing, because her expression changed. "*Oh*, and I've been meaning to tell you: Don't pay any attention to those stupid jokes." She lowered her voice. "You know, the whole stripper business. How juvenile can you get?"

I dug my thumbnail into the side of my finger. "I know," I blurted. Meaning, *Yes, so juvenile, and could we please stop talking about it?*

She glanced toward the door. "Hey, gotta run. Try the white bean soup—it's *fabulous!*"

Oh, crap. Now the big-hair makeup lady is heading our way, and she's loaded down with samples. We are going to be here forever. There is another makeup lady behind the counter who is really pretty, but the big-hair makeup lady is not. I think maybe it should be a job requirement to look good if you're trying to sell makeup. Otherwise it's just too scary.

I wish I didn't care what Rachel thinks of me, but I do. I wish I didn't feel so stupid around her. But I do.

Same day, 4:15 P.M.

Still thinking about the Rachel incident. Kathy would make fun of me if she knew, because she already thinks I give Rachel way too much power. And Kathy hates that. She says it's embarrassing how much I worship her.

But I don't *worship* Rachel. I just care what she thinks, even though I know I'm not supposed to. It's one of those rule things. The popular girls are supposed to bow down to Rachel because they strive to be her, while the not-popular girls—that would be me—are supposed to bow down to her because we know we never will. But behind her back we're supposed to say what a jerk she is, or whatever. This is something that Kathy is very good at.

Only I don't think Rachel *is* a jerk. I mean, yeah, sometimes she says things that aren't exactly nice, like in the cafeteria on Friday when she was showing off her new shirt. Hadley was like, "That is the coolest shirt ever. I love it so much." And Rachel said, "They still have them at Saks if you want one. *Ooo*—but the only ones left are size two. Never mind."

And I remember she made a joke once about how Mika could use two Band-Aids instead of a bra, which made Mika turn bright red. She said it in the hall where everybody could hear, which I admit was pretty bad. But Kathy says stuff like that to me all the time. Not about my bra size, but about how dorky I am or how I really shouldn't wear those jeans or whatever.

Still. Why does Rachel's opinion mean so much to me when she's just a person like the rest of us? Yes, she's beautiful, but so are lots of girls. Mika, for instance, with her dark eyes and jet-black hair. No one would shoo Mika away, but they don't bow down to her like they do to Rachel. Same goes for Hadley. Although Hadley isn't as pretty as Mika or Rachel. She's more just normal, only with really good clothes.

What makes Rachel stand out, I think, is the fact that she's got this incredible confidence about everything she does. Unlike me, who can't even say hello to someone at a restaurant without blushing and mumbling and ducking my head.

After something like that happens, I always think, *If only I could go back and do* this *instead, then everything would be okay.* Like today, I could have tossed out a compliment about Rachel's shoes, for example. Or I could have rolled my eyes when Rachel mentioned the stripper business. "Oh God," I could have groaned. "Isn't it ridiculous?"

All of which is to say that if I could go back to certain moments knowing what I know now, then I would handle them far better. And that is the edge that Rachel already has. She acts like a ninth grader instead of a seventh grader, although she's still living her seventh-grade life.

Monday, September 11, 9:05 A.M.

Megan is so nice! In homeroom she slipped past Ms. Larson and fast-walked to my desk, where she dropped a plastic Baggie tied with a ribbon onto my journal.

"It's a chocolate chip cookie," she whispered. "I made them last night."

"It's *huge,*" I said.

She crouched so that Ms. Larson wouldn't notice her. "I gave one to Kathy, too. Are we going to eat lunch together?"

"Yeah," I said. "Sounds good." I was glad she was being normal, because I'd worried that she'd feel awkward after our late-night talk. That's why I don't talk about private stuff much. It peels back too many layers.

"Girls, you can talk to each other later," Ms. Larson said. She'd lifted her head from her grading. "Megan, get to your own homeroom."

Tuesday, September 12, 8:30 P.M.

Today in social studies, Jeremy rubbed his thumb and fingers together in a cat-calling way and called, "Here, pussy. Here, pussy-pussy!"

Everyone laughed, including me, even though I burned with shame. Pussy, as in Pussycat Palace. One of those horrible, awful words, like others I can't even say. Why aren't there words like that for boys? The ones that exist just aren't as bad, and anyway, guys use them all the time on purpose. They think it makes them sound tough.

Last night at dinner, when I sort of halfway mentioned that Jeremy was giving me a hard time, Dad said that means he likes me. He didn't say it to tease me, like Kathy did at the mall, but he did have a little smile on his face. Like, *I'm a teacher, so I know.*

"No, Dad," I said. "Jeremy's, like, messed up. He lives in a trailer, and he never takes a shower. And his only friend is this guy Pete Nastic, who's always claiming he can do karate moves on people."

"Allison," Mom chided. "Jeremy can't help where he lives. Anyway, there's nothing wrong with living in a trailer."

"He calls me names," I said.

"Like what?" she asked.

I nudged my peas.

Then Dad started going on about how hard life can be for

a kid with a rough home life, and how no, Jeremy shouldn't call me names, but that doesn't mean he's a bad person. "You have no idea what these kids go through," he said. "Jesus, just today one of my fifth graders told me that he and his mom had gotten into a fight, and that his mom had bitten him on the nose."

"What?!" Mom said. She laughed a nervous kind of laugh.

"When I looked closer, I could see teeth marks," Dad said. "Two dents, one over each nostril."

"Dan . . ."

"I know. It's crazy. I told the counselor, and it turns out there's a history of possible abuse already."

"So . . . what's going to happen?" I asked.

Dad rubbed his hand over his face. "Well, Ms. Gray contacted Social Services, and I suspect the kid will be taken away from his mom, at least temporarily."

"And put where?"

"With a relative, hopefully. Or if that doesn't work, in a foster home."

"Oh, Dan, how heartbreaking," Mom said.

"Maybe," Dad said. "Or maybe it'll make things better for him."

He gave me this meaningful look, and I knew I was supposed to, like, connect all that heartbreak to Jeremy. I was supposed to "rise to the occasion," as he was always saying.

Instead, it just made me feel heavy, because now I couldn't even hate Jeremy without feeling guilty about it. If Jeremy wants people to like him, he should stop calling them names.

24

One good thing did come of the whole social studies humiliation deal. I wasn't even going to write about it, because I don't want to build it up in my head, but I can't help it.

It has to do with Rachel Delaney. I guess she saw what was going on with me and Jeremy, and she didn't like it or whatever, because she came over during his "pussy, pussy" routine and looped her arm through mine. "Shut up, Jeremy," she said. "Come on, Alli-cat. I saved you a seat."

"Alli-cat?" Jeremy repeated. "*Alli*-cat?!" He laughed idiotically. "Oh yeah, you better get to your seat, Alli-cat!"

Rachel tugged me away. In a whisper, she said, "It's better than *his* brilliant nickname."

And that was all there was to it. She didn't talk to me for the rest of the class, even though I was right next to her, and she didn't show me the note that got her and Mika giggling uncontrollably. It was totally business as usual, so there's no reason I should keep reliving that one arm-linking moment.

Although she did make a good point. "Here, pussy-pussy" is horrible, but "Alli-cat" isn't so bad.

It's actually kind of cute.

Wednesday, September 13, 4:47 P.M.

I smiled at Rachel in class today, and she smiled back. It's weird how my whole mood can revolve around a small little thing like a smile. But it's different when Rachel smiles at me than when Kathy or even Megan does. It's one of those things that isn't all that fair, because technically Kathy is my best friend and Megan is getting to be a better and better friend, so their smiles should mean more. But Rachel is . . . Rachel. It's just the way it is.

But it was a good day for another reason, too. Because for once, Jeremy found someone else to pick on. Mr. Shakley had stepped out to copy a worksheet, and Jeremy leaped up from his desk and gyrated around the room. He had on a black T-shirt that said HARLEY MAMA in big white letters, and under the words was a picture of a woman in a bikini on a motorcycle. Which, of course, is exactly what I would wear if I was riding a motorcycle.

Anyway, he started singing this really stupid song which went, "I'm too sexy for my shirt, too sexy for my shirt," and everyone cracked up. Well, not me, but a lot of people. Then he grabbed Tory Isaacson's teddy bear off her desk and held it near his crotch, thrusting his hips.

Tory's cheeks got splotchy, and I looked away. Tory's only eleven—she skipped a year—and sometimes I think she's not ready for seventh grade. Even *I* know it's not very smart to bring a teddy bear to school.

I snuck a peek at Rachel, who was laughing along with the others. She covered her mouth like she knew it was bad, but she didn't tell Jeremy to quit.

And now I have to admit something. Part of me liked the fact that Rachel didn't jump to Tory's defense, as she had to mine. I know that sounds terrible.

Mr. Shakley's footsteps echoed in the hall, and Jeremy scrambled for his seat. He threw the bear at Tory.

"What's going on here?" Mr. Shakley demanded. Jeremy

pretended to read his textbook, and Tory clutched her bear to her chest. She didn't have the guts to turn him in.

Friday, September 15, 10:30 P.M.

Tonight Kathy, Megan, and I went to Long John Silver's, where we had a three-hour dinner. Jared MacIlwaine happened to show up, too—evidence that Kathy's been doing some fancy footwork. She turned all bright-eyed and ditzy the moment he sat down, and for some reason she got it into her head to play her hush-puppy game, which goes like this:

hush puppy: "Arf! Arf, arf!" (Kathy's making the hush puppy bound all over the table. She's very cleverly pretending it's a real puppy.)
Kathy: "Hush, puppy, or I'll bite your head off!"
hush puppy: "Arf! Arf, arf!"
Kathy: "*Hush,* puppy, or I'll bite your head off!"
hush puppy: "Arf! Arf, ar—"
Kathy: GLOMP, followed by manic laughter, followed by wet hush puppy spraying everywhere.

There is truly no reason for this game to exist. But Kathy's been playing it for as long as I've known her, and I've no doubt she'll be playing it when she's ninety, to the horror of all the other nursing-home residents.

Anyway, during the third round of hush-puppy hysteria, a glob of spitty hush puppy flew from Kathy's mouth and landed on the lens of Jared's glasses. So for the rest of the evening Kathy was either hiding her face and giggling, or shooting us anguished glances when Jared wasn't looking. Anguished glances that weren't truly anguished, because Jared snort-laughed when it happened and slugged Kathy on the shoulder, saying, "Good one, McConagal."

It *was* funny, but it wasn't, like, the most hilarious thing on earth. I had to work to get into the total spaz mood of it all.

Later, when Kathy and Jared were making moony eyes over a Sierra Mist, Megan and I splintered off and chatted on our own. Not about anything big—just school and clothes and TV shows. Stuff like that. She was telling me about this cute pair of pants she'd found on eBay when a lady walked into the restaurant, paused, and wrinkled her nose.

"Heavens, what is that *smell?*" she asked.

I guess there was kind of a fried fish smell in the air, although I'd totally gotten used to it. After all, we were in Long John Silver's.

But without missing a beat, Megan cringed and said, "Oh, that's just me." She didn't mean for the lady to hear, but one look at the lady's pinchy-squinchy face told us she did. Megan and I started laughing and couldn't stop, and this time I didn't have to work at it at all.

Sunday, September 17, 11:01 A.M.

There is seriously something wrong with me. I've spent the last thirty-five minutes staring at myself in Mom's makeup mirror, and I've discovered that my nose has all these weird little dots on it. I wouldn't have noticed if I hadn't used the mirror's magnifier function, and if I hadn't adjusted the dial to DAYLIGHT, which makes the mirror really bright. But now that I *have* noticed, they're all I can see. They're not zits—they're teeny tiny and kind of whitish, although I'm pretty sure they're not whiteheads either. If I step back two feet from the mirror, I can't see them anymore, which is good because it means that people in my everyday life probably can't see them, either. But I know they're there, and they're freaking me out.

I think I need those nose strip thingies I saw on a commercial, where the girl puts one on her nose, and when she pulls it off, it's covered with little stalactites of dirt. I think whoever invented those strips is very smart. It's like, did I know I was walking through life under a crust of gunk? No, I did not. But now that I do, I'm determined to do something about it.

Same day, 1:15 P.M.

Oh good God. So I'm back from Eckerd's, where I RAN INTO JEREMY WEBSTER WHILE I HAD A BOX OF NOSE STRIPS IN MY HAND!!!

I mean, okay. Breathe. It could have been worse. It could have been a box of, well, a box of something else I might have been buying in my hand. Not that I would have been buying that particular thing at Eckerd's. That's a mom kind of thing to buy, since she's thirty-eight and beyond caring.

But still. When I saw Jeremy, my whole body heated up and I whipped the box behind my back. I know they were just nose strips. I know that. But for him to catch me with them made me feel . . . I don't know. Like it was out there for the whole world to see, the fact that I care what I look like.

"Hey," I said. "How's it going?" My heart whammed against my ribs.

He didn't respond, and I hated myself for even trying. But then I noticed that *he* was blushing.

"Not bad," he said. "Just, you know, hanging out."

"Yeah. Me, too."

He stood there.

"Well . . . see you," I said.

He straightened his shoulders and did this stupid point-and-wink move. Then he sauntered over to the candy aisle.

I hovered by the magazines until he left, then paid for my nose strips and hurried home. But I haven't used one, because now it's all wrong. I wish I'd gotten Mom to drive me to Kmart instead. I wish I were the type of person who could laugh it off, like, "Nose strips? Yeah, baby. Refine those pores!"

THEY'RE JUST STUPID NOSE STRIPS. WHAT IS MY PROBLEM?!

I wish I were anyone but me.

Monday, September 18, lunch

No comments from Jeremy in social studies, so I'm thinking that maybe I'm safe. Boys aren't always good at noticing those things, anyway. Maybe he thought I had a box of Band-Aids or something.

It so sucks to be worried all the time, afraid that someone is going to see the parts of me I'm trying to hide. I wish I could trust myself to be cool. Only, who am I kidding? I'm *not* cool, and that's what I'm always scared people are going to find out.

Rachel does not have this problem. I'm beginning to think that Megan doesn't, either. Today she showed up in this really embarrassing T-shirt. It had one of those big-eyed, cutesy cats on it that's supposed to make everyone go "awww." It was a T-shirt like your grandmother might give you, which, in fact, was exactly the case.

Megan was like, "I know. It's horrible, isn't it?" And then she laughed, which made me and Kathy laugh, too. Carter Hunt passed us in the hall and said, totally sarcastically, "Nice shirt," and Megan shot back, "You know it!"

"Did you bring something to change into?" Kathy asked.

"No," Megan said. "My grandmom sent this to me because she knows I love cats. It was really sweet of her."

Her eyes met mine, and I knew she was thinking about her own cat, Fred. I guess she does hide some stuff after all.

In other news, Kathy and Jared are officially an item. He just loped over to our table and presented Kathy with a mangled fork, its handle bent and its tines jutting out every which way. According to him, the fork symbolizes man's struggle against the herd.

"The herd?" I said. "What herd?"

Jared grabbed a regular fork and stood it and the mangled fork side by side. He gestured with the regular fork, its tines straight and even. "Herd mentality," he pronounced. He gestured with the mangled fork. "One of a kind. Get it?"

I didn't. "So . . . Kathy is the mangled fork?"

"Well, you're sure not," Kathy said. She laughed, which made me mad.

"*I'm* not part of the herd," I said.

"But you want to be," she shot back.

I could feel my face get hot. My gaze happened to flit to Rachel's table, and unfortunately Kathy noticed.

"You are *so* busted!" she said, gloating. "Ha!"

Rachel turned to look—along with some other kids—and I wanted to sink through the floor.

"I have no idea what you're talking about," I said.

Kathy patted my arm. "Don't worry, Alli. We love you anyway."

Same day, English

Just because somebody—namely, Kathy—isn't part of the popular crowd, that doesn't make her special by default. It doesn't mean she, like, *chose* to be different.

Anyway, who wants to be a mangled fork?

Wednesday, September 20, 10:24 P.M.

Aye-yai-yai. I need to go to bed, but I'm too wound up. Today in social studies, Mr. Shakley announced that it was time to start preparing for the History Fair, which is this big-deal nighttime event that the whole school attends.

"In groups of two, you will select a topic and research it thoroughly," Mr. Shakley told us. "Along with a ten-page report, you will construct a project of some sort—a diorama, a model—which you will display at the fair. Any questions?"

Hadley's hand shot up. "Can we work in groups of three instead of two?"

"There will be one group of three, since we have an odd number of people in the class," Mr. Shakley said.

"Yes," Hadley whispered, making a fist and pulling it in at her side. She grinned at Rachel and Mika.

"Anything else? No? In that case . . ." Mr. Shakley pulled a piece of loose-leaf paper from his drawer. "Listen for your names, and then I'll give you time to get together with your partner and start talking about what you want to do."

Hadley straightened up in alarm. "You picked our partners for us?"

Mr. Shakley looked at her over the top of the list. "Of course. Now pay attention. Gini and Maggie, you two will work together. Matt, you work with Amy Carlisle, and Amy Peterson, you're with Stuart Miller. Seeta al-Sarhi, you're with—"

Hadley squeezed her eyes shut and crossed her fingers. I tried to act casual, half hoping I'd be paired with Aaron Sarmiento. But as long as I wasn't put with Jeremy, I was okay with pretty much anyone.

"Let's see," Mr. Shakley said when he was about halfway down the list. "Rachel, I'd like for you to form a group with Elizabeth and Mika."

Behind me, Rachel and Mika squealed. Hadley looked stricken.

Hadley got assigned to Tory Isaacson, the girl with the teddy bear, while Aaron and Chris Floyd were paired together. Jeremy was put with Mark Balkin, a computer geek who everyone knew would end up doing the whole project.

"And Alli," Mr. Shakley said, "I'd like you to pair with Maxine."

I let out my breath. Maxine was brainy but nice, and even though I was disappointed about Aaron, I knew she and I would work well together.

Mr. Shakley folded the piece of paper and stuck it in his grade book. "Take the rest of the period to start talking about your projects," he said. "Remember, you'll need to—" He broke off. "Yes, Maxine?"

"Um, I don't know if I should be put in a group or not, because my family's moving," she said. "My mom got a job in Chicago."

"What? In Chicago?"

"We leave at the end of this week." She glanced at me apologetically.

"Well, Alli, I guess that leaves you stranded," he said. He pulled his list out once more. "Why don't you pair up with Mika, and that'll leave Rachel and Elizabeth to still be partners. All right? Now gather your books—" He sighed. "Yes, Rachel?"

"No offense," Rachel said, "but couldn't Mika and I be partners, and let Elizabeth be with Alli?"

I kept my eyes on my desk.

"No, no, no," Mr. Shakley said. "If I let you switch partners, then everyone's going to want to switch. Now listen, we've got five minutes left in class, so everybody get together with your partners." He stared at us, then threw his hands in the air. "Go!"

I glanced at Mika. She, Rachel, and Hadley were deep in conversation. Mr. Shakley approached them, and Mika slid out of her seat before he could scold her. I opened my textbook and acted busy.

"So . . ." Mika said, standing beside me.

"You can be Rachel's partner if you want to," I told her. "I don't care."

She hesitated, then flipped her hair over her shoulder and sat down. "Do you have any ideas? For our project?"

I lifted my eyebrows. She didn't have to pretend to be into it.

Mika sighed. She tried to subtly check on Rachel and Hadley.

"Well, we have to think of something," she said.

"I know."

Mr. Shakley left Gini and Maggie's desks and moved on to us. "Okay, you two, what have you decided to focus on?" he asked.

"Um," Mika began, "we haven't exactly—"

"Surely you have some general thoughts. Alli?"

I glanced at the page in front of me. "Um, we thought we'd do . . . Pocahontas, and, um . . ."

"And how her rescue of John Smith was maybe a setup?" Mika filled in. She briefly met my eyes, then plowed on. "How maybe she and her dad planned the whole thing?"

"Ah," Mr. Shakley said. "An issue you can dig your teeth into. Keep up the good work, girls."

When he was out of earshot, I asked, "Is that true? About Pocahontas and John Smith?"

Mika shrugged. "Some people think so."

"How do you know?"

"Some friend of my mom's gave me a book about her for my birthday. She was all 'Every girl needs a positive role model,' blah, blah, blah."

"Oh," I said. I must have looked confused, because Mika rolled her eyes.

"You know, because Pocahontas was different from the settlers. The whole 'colors of the wind' thing."

"Oh," I said again.

"So, when should we meet?" she asked. "You could come to my house if you want. Maybe Saturday afternoon?"

"Uh, sure."

She scribbled something in her notebook and tore it off. "Here's my address."

And now, nine hours later, I'm here in bed with my nightshirt pulled over my knees, and I know I should be freaking out about spending an entire afternoon with Mika Satomi. And I am. But I'm also thinking about what she said when I asked her about Pocahontas. Because yeah, Mika's Japanese, but other than her being popular, I never thought of her as being different from anybody else.

Same night, 10:54 P.M.

Oh. Kathy and Megan are both in Mr. Shakley's second-period social studies class, and they got assigned to be partners. I guess I'm a little jealous, but not as much as I would have thought.

Today after school, Kathy, Megan, and I went to the mall. Kathy's sister, Leslie, drove us. When she saw me, she said, "Hey hey, it's the stripper of the seventh grade! Going to buy yourself some new pasties at Wet 'n Wild?"

I climbed into the car. With Leslie, just like with Kathy, it was better not to let on when something bugged you.

"What are pasties?" Kathy asked.

Leslie waited while Megan shut the back door, then reversed out of the drive. In a talk-show host's voice, she said, "Student by day, stripper by night. The perfect cover. What other secrets lie hidden in the heart of this mysterious young girl?"

I scrunched my toes inside my sneakers.

"I said, what are pasties?" Kathy demanded.

"Those shiny things striptease dancers wear on their boobs," Leslie said. "Sometimes they have tassels."

"Omigod," Kathy said. "Are you, Alli? Are you going to get some pasties?"

I knew they were teasing, but I wished they would shut up. "Yeah, Kathy. That's exactly what I'm going to do. Probably hot-pink ones."

"Ha!" Kathy crowed. "Me, too, only I'm going to get gold. And one of those G-string things to go with it."

"You, a stripper?" Leslie said. "Everyone in the audience would run screaming out of the club."

"What? No, they wouldn't!"

"Uh, hate to remind you, Kathy, but strippers are supposed to be *pretty*. People have to want to see what's underneath."

Kathy twisted toward the window. She was no longer laughing. "I hate you," she said.

In the backseat, Megan's eyes met mine. I gave a tiny shrug to say, *I know. Just keep quiet.* The whole car filled with uncomfortableness.

Megan leaned forward. "Don't worry, Kathy. You can strip for me anytime."

"Ooo!" Leslie said. "Is that how it is, then?"

"Uh-huh," Megan deadpanned. "Me and Kathy and Alli. Ménage à trois."

Kathy turned from the window and shoved Megan's shoulder. "Sick!" she said, giggling. "That is so gross!"

At the mall, the three of us went to the Limited because Kathy needed some new jeans. She picked out about ten thousand pairs and dragged us with her to the dressing room, where she asked our opinion on each. For one pair, she had to lie down on the floor to get the zipper up. I've kind of grown out of the whole tight jeans thing, although I do want my jeans to look good. But I don't know why she'd want a pair that would make her so uncomfortable.

"What about these?" she said, pushing herself up and looking at herself in the mirror. She turned around and peered over her shoulder. "Do they make my butt look fat?"

"No, they make your butt look flat," Megan said. "They make it so that you have no butt."

"Is that a good thing?" Kathy asked.

"You want to have *some* butt," Megan said. "The first pair looked better."

Kathy unsnapped the jeans and wiggled out of them. They left a red mark around her waist.

"Back in Boulder, my mom worked with a woman who had surgery because she thought her butt was too flat," Megan went on. "It was like a face-lift, only it was a butt-lift instead."

"Nuh-uh," Kathy said.

"Yeah-huh," Megan said. "Big butts are in."

I thought of something Jeremy had said during social studies earlier that day, so I told them about it. How we were supposed to be working on our projects, when all of a sudden Jeremy hopped onto his chair and started shaking his butt.

"He was going, 'Boo-*tay!* I say I got some boo-*tay!*'"

"*Why?*" Megan said.

"What did Mr. Shakley do?" Kathy said.

"He told him to get back to work, and Jeremy goes, 'But I am working! We're doing the Spanish pirates, and it says right here that they called their treasure "booty"!' So Mr. Shakley goes, 'Get off the chair this instant. Do it, Webster, or you'll be pushing Georgia until *I* get tired.'"

"Pushing Georgia?" Kathy repeated. "What is that supposed to mean?" She reached for the first pair of jeans and slipped them back on.

"Push-ups," I said. "He told Jeremy to do twenty, but Jeremy kept arguing, and so it turned into thirty."

"Ahh," Megan said. "Push-ups. Pushing Georgia. Clever."

I thought about Jeremy up at the front of the room, huffing away with his face beet red and his bangs matted with sweat. At first some of the kids had laughed, but Mr. Shakley kept counting and Jeremy kept puffing and pretty soon everyone grew silent. Like, abnormally silent.

"Do you think Mr. Shakley would ever make a girl do push-ups?" I asked.

"No way," Megan said. She frowned. "No. No way."

Kathy zipped up the jeans and craned around to examine her butt again. "What did Rachel have to say about all this? And Mika?"

My muscles tightened.

"They didn't say anything," I said. "At least not to me."

"Oh, too bad. I thought maybe you were in their 'in' circle now, since you're Mika's partner and everything."

"Shut up," I said.

"What is it with you, Kathy?" Megan said. "You're always going on about how Alli is obsessed with them or whatever. But really I think it's *you* who's obsessed."

"Oh, please," Kathy said.

"Anyway, Alli wouldn't want to be in their 'in' circle," Megan said. "She's way smarter than that."

Kathy burst out laughing. "Hate to burst your bubble, but no, she's not. She'd drop us in a second if Rachel said the word."

I purposely ignored her. Hoping nothing showed on my face, I turned to Megan. "What do you mean, I'm too smart for that?"

Megan shrugged. "I don't know. Mika's okay, I guess. But Hadley's a jerk."

I bit my lip. Hadley was a bit of a jerk. She was one of the kids who'd been laughing the loudest when Jeremy first got in trouble.

"And Rachel . . . I don't know," Megan went on. "I know you like her, Alli, but she seems pretty full of herself."

"Like how?"

"Just the way she dresses, and how she always has to look so perfect, and how she'll, like, tell other girls that they need to redo their highlights and crap like that."

"Who did she tell to redo her highlights? I never heard her tell anyone that."

"She said it to Samantha Miller in the bathroom the other day. She was like, 'Your bone structure is all wrong for chunky highlights. And you picked the completely wrong color.'"

"Maybe she was trying to be helpful."

"I don't think so. It's weird, Alli. It's as if she can say whatever she wants, and no one will stop her."

I didn't know how to respond to that. I wanted to say, *Yeah, well, Kathy treats me the exact same way. Why don't you get all over* her *about it?* I stared at the dressing-room floor, which was littered with those plastic thingies that come off clothes.

"But I could be wrong," Megan said.

"You're not," Kathy said. She turned in a circle so we could admire her jeans. "So these are the ones? You're sure?"

"Absolutely," Megan said.

Kathy squinted at her reflection, then grabbed the butt-squishing jeans from the floor. She tossed them to me.

"You should try them, Alli," she said. "You're so skinny, I bet they'd look terrific."

Spent the last half hour IM-ing with Megan. Here's what she said:

> **megawatt: so guess who wants to drive halfway across the country to visit me?**
>
> alli-cat12: who?

(I changed my screen name last week, only "alli-cat" was already taken, so I had to stick in my age. Still, it's a thousand times cuter than "allisongrace.")

> **megawatt: my father. +barf+ he's totally doing it out of guilt, which is ridiculous cuz i have no desire to see him.**
>
> alli-cat12: u don't miss him? not even a teeny bit?

There was a fairly long pause before Megan answered, so I took the opportunity to smooth on a nose strip. I finally worked up my nerve to try one, because I want to look my best when I go to Mika's tomorrow.

> **megawatt: a teeny bit, maybe. but what am i supposed to do about my mom?**
>
> alli-cat12: what do u mean?
>
> **megawatt: i'm afraid it'll hurt her feelings if he comes. i heard her tell my aunt that in her opinion, dad lost his fathering privileges when he moved out of the house.**

alli-cat12: ouch

megawatt: she didn't know i was listening.

alli-cat12: i guess she's really pissed at him, huh?

megawatt: wouldn't u be?

megawatt: sorry. it's just no fun being in the middle.

alli-cat12: hey, i know—tell him to bring your cat! then
no one will get their feelings hurt, because OF
COURSE you'd be excited to see fred. and if a little
of that excitement slips over onto your dad, well,
who cares? it's brilliant!

megawatt: yeah, except for 1 thing.

alli-cat12: what?

**megawatt: dad and fred in the same car for two days? i
don't think so.**

alli-cat12: oh.

**megawatt: i wish none of this had happened. i wish
there was some way i could go back and change
things. do u ever think things like that? like, if only u
could do things differently then everything would be
perfect?**

megawatt: alli? are u there?

megawatt: alli!!!

alli-cat12: i'm here, i'm here! sorry!

megawatt: what happened? where did u go?

alli-cat12: nowhere! i was right here.

I didn't want to tell her I'd been taking off my nose strip. But
I *had* to take it off, or it would have turned to cement. I felt

guilty, though, because I really did care about what she was saying.

alli-cat12: anyway, YES. i always wish i could go back in time. like with the great underwear fiasco, for example.

megawatt: hmm. yeah, i can see that.

alli-cat12: but megan, u didn't make your dad take off with his secretary.

megawatt: i guess

alli-cat12: it still sucks, tho. if i were God, i'd give everybody 1 do-over button to use however they wanted. wouldn't that be awesome?

megawatt: if only something like that really existed.

alli-cat12: altho i'd need like 5000 of them. 1 for every day of my life.

megawatt: why do u say that? u never screw up.

alli-cat12: ahem, the underwear incident? must i mention that again?

megawatt: that's 1 thing. ONE.

alli-cat12: anyway, kathy sure thinks i do. she gets on my case about everything. even stuff i have no control over, like being mika's partner for the history fair. and all that stuff about being obsessed with rachel, which i'm totally not.

megawatt: she does kinda go on about that. why is that, do u think? is it cuz she's jealous?

alli-cat12: yes. but that's no excuse for being mean.

megawatt: but, alli . . .

alli-cat12: what?

megawatt: i don't know. i wouldn't even say anything if u hadn't brought it up, but

megawatt: never mind.

alli-cat12: what?!! TELL ME!

megawatt: sometimes i don't get why u 2 r even friends, that's all.

alli-cat12: we're NOT friends, which is exactly what i've been trying to tell kathy! i barely know her!

megawatt: no, not u and rachel. u and kathy.

I felt really weird when she said that. Dumb at first, like, "Duh, of course she didn't think you were friends with Rachel." And then all of a sudden jittery, because I wasn't sure I wanted to go where she was going.

megawatt: alli?

alli-cat12: ur friends with her 2, u know. kathy, i mean.

megawatt: but only cuz u r. why do u let her treat u the way she does?

alli-cat12: what? i don't "let" her do anything. anyway, easy for u to say. she never bugs u about stuff.

megawatt: yes she does. only i tell her to stop. u just get all quiet, and so she keeps going and going and going.

I took my hands off the keyboard. I'd only complained about Kathy because I'd expected Megan to be on my side, not to gang up on me.

megawatt: i don't mean that in a BAD way. u've just gotta stand up for yourself sometimes.

alli-cat12: yeah, whatever

megawatt: alli? r u mad? i'm afraid ur all mad now.

alli-cat12: i've g2g. mom's calling me for dinner.

megawatt: ok, but just don't take what i said the wrong way. i didn't mean to make u upset.

alli-cat12: i'm not upset. i've g2g, that's all.

megawatt: all right. well, thanks for listening about all that dad stuff. bye!

Same night, 6:43 P.M.

I like Megan. I really do. She's nice and she's funny and she never does anything to hurt my feelings, at least not on purpose. And it made me feel good when she said she was only friends with Kathy because I was friends with Kathy. Because what that meant was, "*You.* The real person I'm friends with is *you.*" (Although it made me feel a little bad for Kathy, too, which is dumb, since Kathy's been getting on my nerves so much recently.)

But Megan's new this year. She doesn't know how complicated things are, how before now I didn't have the option *not* to be friends with Kathy. So sure, it's easy for Megan to say, "Oh, you should stand up for yourself. You shouldn't let her treat you that way."

But instead of helping, it just makes me feel like a loser.

Same night, 7:05 P.M.

Just for the record, the nose strip worked just like the commercials said it would. When I peeled it off, it was covered with little bitty stalactites of nose dirt. Dirt that *had been* part of me, but that was ripped from my skin and is now clinging to the nose strip.

Who knew?

Saturday, September 23, 11:43 A.M.

I'm supposed to be at Mika's in fifteen minutes, and my stomach's in knots. I know that's ridiculous, but I can't help it. Mika's not Rachel, but she *is* Mika—and she *is* Rachel's best friend.

I don't know how to talk to her. I don't know how to BE around her. She's too beautiful. Too glossy breezy perfect. And no, I'm not obsessing, because worrying is different from obsessing.

When I first woke up, I was actually a little excited. Because maybe I'd . . . I don't know. Not be a total idiot. And maybe Mika and I would start to be friends. Not "best bud" kind of friends, but "hey, cute shirt" kind of friends, the kind who'd smile when we saw each other in the halls. And in social studies, if I sat next to her, it wouldn't be some enormous sin. She'd be like, "Alli, hi. Did you have a good weekend?"

But I don't feel excited anymore.

I feel like I'm going to throw up.

Same day, Mika's room

Well, I was right to worry. I'm sitting at Mika's desk and I'm hyperventilating and as soon as she comes back upstairs, I'm telling her I'm out of here. Because no way am I going to be here when THEY arrive. No freaking way.

It's sad, because until now, things were going so well. Like, *super* well. Better than I expected.

"You must be Allison," Mrs. Satomi exclaimed when I first arrived. Mika was nowhere to be seen. "Would you like some tea?"

"Oh, no thanks," I said.

"Just a little," Mrs. Satomi said.

She poured me a cup from a pale blue teapot. We sat silently for a few minutes, and then Mrs. Satomi said, "Perhaps Mika had to stay late today."

"Um . . . where is she?"

"Japanese language school. Every Saturday morning."

"Oh." In my mind I saw Dad's funky brown T-shirt, the one with the Japanese writing on it. At least, I think it's Japanese. "That would be so neat to know another language."

"I wish you would tell Mika that," Mrs. Satomi said. She sighed. "Sometimes I worry that Mika is not interested in learning Japanese. Sometimes I worry that she does not—"

The front door banged shut. "Mom?" Mika called. "I'm home! Is Alli here?" She rushed into the living room. "Oh, hey! Sorry I'm late." She spotted my teacup. *"Mom."*

Mrs. Satomi frowned. "Mika . . ."

Mika dropped her eyes. "Come on, Alli. Let's go upstairs."

Mika and I worked on our project for two hours. At first I was pretty quiet, because just being here in her room with all her stuff made me nervous. She has posters of bands I know nothing about, and all over the room are pictures of her and Rachel and Hadley, grinning and hugging and looking gorgeous. Well, except for Hadley.

48

But after a while I threw out some ideas about how to organize our paper, and Mika acted like what I said made sense. She drew her eyebrows together while she listened, and every so often she'd say, "Yeah. Yeah, okay."

Then we started talking about what it would be like to live back in the olden days, which is weird, I know. But Mika brought it up, not me. She'd been reading out loud about Pocahontas bringing food to the settlers, and she stopped and put down the book.

"Sometimes I wish I lived back then, you know?" she said. "Like in *Little House on the Prairie*, when everyone lived in log cabins."

"You used to read the *Little House on the Prairie* books?" I asked.

Mika faltered. "Well, only when I was little. My mom gave them to me for my birthday when I was, like, six, and I—"

"I loved those books," I interrupted. "And I know what you mean. They made me want to live in a log cabin, too."

"Are you serious?"

I nodded.

"You know how Pa would kill a hog every summer?" Mika said. "I wanted to make a balloon out of the hog's bladder, just like Laura."

"And fry the tail over the fire until it made crackling sounds?"

"Yeah! And make candy in the winter by pouring molasses onto a plate of snow."

We looked at each other and started giggling. Inside I was like, *Yes. I'm doing it. I'm sitting here talking to Mika and we're actually having FUN.*

Then the telephone rang. From downstairs, Mrs. Satomi called, "Mika? For you!"

Mika reached for her phone. "Hello?" she said. "Oh, hi! Wait, stop talking at the same time. I can't understand you!"

My giddiness dried up. I picked at a hole in my jeans and tried to look casual.

"You *what?*" Mika said. "No way. No *way!*" She pressed her hand over the receiver. "Rachel got her belly button pierced," she told me. She clutched the phone back to her ear. "Okay, see you then. Don't mess with it or it'll get infected!"

She hung up. "Omigod, her dad is going to kill her."

"He is?"

"He's, like, superstrict and gets mad all the time over stuff that's totally stupid. He thinks piercings are trashy."

I frowned. She was going too fast. "So . . . what will she do? Is she going to hide it from him?"

"I don't know. We can ask her when she gets here. You don't mind, do you?"

My heart pounded. What was I supposed to say? *Yippee! I can't wait!*

"Crap," Mika said, "this room is such a mess." She snatched a Ding Dong wrapper from the floor and dumped it in the trash, then picked up our Coke cans and cradled them in her arms. "I'm going to go throw these in the recycling bin. Do you think you could grab our books and put them on my desk?"

"Uh, sure."

"Thanks."

She dashed out of the room, leaving me alone in the middle of the floor. I straightened up her desk and loaded my backpack. (All except for this journal, of course. Duh.) And as soon as she comes back, I'm taking off.

Rachel and Mika and Hadley . . . and me?

There's just no way.

Same night, back at home

Okay, so I didn't leave after all. (Well, obviously I left eventually. Otherwise I'd still be there. I'd be like, "Hi again, Mrs. Satomi! Guess I'm living here now. Got any spare pajamas?") But I didn't end up dashing out like a coward, and I *think* I'm glad, although I'm not entirely positive.

"What are you doing?" Mika had asked when she saw me with my stuff all packed up. "You're not leaving, are you?"

I mumbled something about how much homework I had, and Mika gave me a look.

"Alli," she said. "They're not going to bite."

"It's not *that*," I said.

Downstairs, the doorbell rang.

"Stay," Mika coaxed. She glanced toward the hall. "But don't mention where I was this morning."

"You mean Japanese language school? Why not?"

"Because I hate it. It's not like Rachel and Hadley don't know about it, because they do, but the whole thing is totally embarrassing."

Footsteps pounded on the stairs. My brain locked up, and I inched back against Mika's desk.

"Ta-da!" Rachel said, striking a pose in Mika's doorway. Her cheeks were flushed and her eyes were bright. "What do you think?"

Mika squealed. She was suddenly more animated than she'd been all afternoon. "Omigod! I can't believe you did it!"

Rachel's shirt hit right above her waist, and there, looped through her belly button, was a shiny silver hoop. Behind Rachel stood Hadley. She looked pleased, as if she'd earned points for being present at the piercing when Mika wasn't.

"Did it hurt?" Mika asked. "Did they make you bring in a permission slip?"

"If they did, I would have had to forge it," Rachel said. She spotted me in the corner. "Alli! I didn't know you were here. Come see my belly button ring."

I unstuck myself from my hiding place. Rachel's stomach was flat and tan, and the silver hoop gleamed against her skin.

"Um . . . looks good," I said.

"Thanks," Rachel said. She smiled.

"So they just let you do it, no questions asked?" Mika said.

Rachel walked over to Mika's bed, where she dropped down on the mattress. She slid her backpack off her shoulder. "I told the lady I was sixteen. I guess she believed me."

"I was like, 'Just be cool. Just be cool,'" Hadley said. "And I guess both of us being there made it seem better, because people are always telling me I look old for my age. I thought about getting mine done, too, but mainly I just wanted to be there for Rachel. In case she fainted."

Rachel said, "Sure, Hadley. Whatever you say."

Mika snorted back a laugh. Hadley turned red.

Rachel dug around in her backpack and pulled out a bag of Swedish fish. She took a few and handed the bag to Mika. "Here."

Mika shook three into her palm. "Did it hurt? Do you have to twist it or use peroxide or anything?"

"She has to dab it with alcohol every night for two weeks," Hadley said. "I told the lady I'd remind her." She held up her outstretched hand, and Mika tossed her the Swedish fish. She dumped out a big clump.

"Don't eat them *all*," Rachel said. "Save some for Alli."

"That's okay," I said.

Hadley glared at me, even though I hadn't done a thing.

"What about your dad?" Mika asked. She gestured at Rachel's belly. "He's going to see it if you go home like that."

Rachel shrugged. "If he does, he does."

"She brought a sweatshirt," Hadley said. "It's in her backpack."

"He's going to kill you if he finds out," Mika said.

Rachel flopped back on the bed, hands behind her head so that her shirt inched higher over her ribs. "You guys have been working on your project, right? You kicking some social studies butt?"

My eyes flew to Mika. I didn't know if Rachel was making fun of us or not.

"It's going okay," Mika said. "We haven't really been working that hard on it."

"Well, you should," Rachel said. "Got to get those A's."

"If you say so," Mika said.

I half smiled, unsure what was going on. It was a teasing kind of thing, I knew that much, but I had the sense it could quickly turn into something else.

Rachel turned her head to look at me. "What about Jeremy? Is he still giving you a hard time?"

"About what?" I asked.

For some reason that amused her. "It's so uncalled for, all those 'pussy-pussy' remarks. It's total sexual harassment."

Heat crept up my face. "He probably just wants attention."

"He's a slime," Hadley said.

"He needs to learn some respect," Rachel said. "Want us to beat him up for you?"

I blinked. Then I said, "Oh yeah, would you please?" I strived for the same tough-but-bored tone Rachel had used on me, and she laughed in surprise. I felt a surge of pride. I'd held my own. I'd thrown out a (somewhat) witty remark, and it had worked.

"Anyway, it's more my fault than his," I said. "I, like, don't know how to stand up to him."

I heard the words come out of my mouth, and I waited without breathing for Rachel's response.

"Why?" Rachel said. "He's nobody."

"Yeah, but . . . so am I. Ever since last year, when I missed all that school." I couldn't believe I was saying all this, except that Rachel's attention made me want more.

"Oh, that's *right*," Rachel said. "You were sick or something, weren't you?"

"You got really fat," Hadley said. She snickered.

"No, she didn't, and anyway, she's not now, so shut up,"

Rachel said. She unfolded herself from the bed and came over to me. "Jeremy's a loser. You don't know how to deal with him, that's all."

"If I were you, I would," I said. "You know how to handle everything."

My braveness amazed me. But the corner of Rachel's mouth turned up, and I could tell she was pleased.

She put her arm around my shoulders. "Well, then I guess I'll have to teach you."

Sunday, September 24, 4:25 P.M.

Kathy and Megan came over today, and it was weird seeing the two of them after being at Mika's yesterday. I kind of wanted to tell them about it, but I knew they wouldn't understand.

Anyway, Kathy was in a makeover mood, so that's what we did. Mom says that makeup is all about hope, that women wear makeup because they think that by covering up their imperfections, they'll be magically transformed into someone new. She acts as if that's a bad thing—not that I see her going au naturel.

Personally, I'm kind of wishy-washy about makeup. I like the way it makes me look, but I don't wear any to school. One, because Mom would kill me, and two, because I wouldn't want anyone to notice. I guess it makes me feel as if I'm trying too hard, and then I worry that everyone will *see* that I'm trying too hard, and that makes me way too self-conscious.

But Kathy loves makeup. She has an entire pink plastic toolbox of foundations, eyeliners, and lipsticks, and the three of us went all out. Cashmere Beige eyeliner to bring out Megan's eyes and

Sheer Apricot blush to give her that sun-kissed look. For Kathy, Mom's Pale Honey foundation to hide her freckles, although Megan told her not to. "Your freckles are adorable," she told her.

As for me, I got busy with Kathy's powder sheets, which are these cool little Kleenex-y things that you use to blot up oil on your forehead and nose. Then I swooped on some Smoky Gray eyeliner and black mascara. Oh so mysterious.

HOWEVER. Even though I wasn't planning on talking about Rachel, I must have snuck in a few remarks without meaning to. And Kathy called me on it. She was uncapping a lipstick called Ravishing Blackcurrant, and without thinking, I said, "Rachel wears that color. She says you have to have olive skin tones to pull it off."

Kathy lowered the lipstick. "Oh, does she?" she said in an unnecessarily snotty tone.

"What is that supposed to mean?" I asked.

"When did you see her anyway, that she would have mentioned what lipstick she wears?"

I was so not in the mood to have Kathy jump all over me. Plus I felt self-conscious knowing that Megan was there watching. But maybe that was good, because it kind of made me feel stronger inside of myself, like I wasn't going to let Kathy get away with it.

I lifted my chin and told them that we'd hung out yesterday, me and Rachel and Mika and Hadley. I told them that we'd talked about lots of things, not just lipstick.

Kathy looked at Megan like, *See?*

"What?" I said.

"Nothing, just that now it makes sense," Kathy said. "'Rachel is so funny.' 'Rachel *loves* Swedish fish.' And 'Rachel pierced her belly button, you know. Her dad's going to kill her.' You have no idea how stupid you sound."

Floored, I turned to Megan.

She fooled with a tube of concealer. "I don't want to get in the middle."

"Which is her nice way of saying I'm right," Kathy said.

I could feel my cheeks burn. My chest tightened up as if I'd done something to be embarrassed of, which I *hadn't*.

I told Kathy that she was making a mountain out of a molehill, which was something my third-grade teacher used to say.

Kathy raised her chin. She didn't look the least bit apologetic.

"This is stupid," I finally said. "Let's finish our makeovers."

But after that it wasn't the same. And the Ravishing Blackcurrant was way too dark against Kathy's pale skin, only she wouldn't admit it, so for the rest of the afternoon she looked like a little kid playing dress-up. If anyone should have been embarrassed, it was her.

Monday, September 25, study hall

Megan found me before social studies and told me some great news: She and her mom are renting a house!

"Megan, that's awesome!" I said.

"I know," Megan said. "Dad called and said he really is coming to visit, and Mom freaked out because she couldn't stand the thought of him seeing our dumpy apartment. So she put down one month's rent on a really cute two-bedroom."

"See? So something good *did* come out of it."

"And here's the best part. The landlady says cats are okay, so Mom says eventually we can get a kitten!"

I slapped Megan a high five. "Yes! When do you move in?"

"The lease goes into effect this Thursday, so we'll probably start moving this weekend."

"Megan, that rocks," I said. I would have said more, but right then Mika pushed her way through a clump of kids and grabbed my arm.

"Mika, hey!" I said.

"Hi," she said. She smiled at Megan. "Hi, Meadow."

"It's Megan," Megan said.

Mika widened her eyes. "Really? I thought it was Meadow."

Megan looked at her like, *It's my name. I'm pretty sure I'm right.* "Nope. It's Megan."

"*Megan*. God, I'm so sorry." She turned to me. "Alli, I need your help with that bibliography thingie we're supposed to turn in."

"Oh," I said. "Okay, I'll be right there."

"You have to come now. We only have two minutes." She started tugging me away.

"I'll see you at lunch," I called to Megan. "All right? We can talk more then!" I waved in an overly cheery sort of way, but Megan didn't wave back.

Same day, French

What was I supposed to do, tell Mika no? Our bibliography counts for ten percent of our grade. It's important.

Does Megan want me to fail?!!

Mika and Rachel saw me before class started and waved me over. They were standing outside Mr. Shakley's door and giggling. Happiness spurted up inside me, and I hurried toward them.

"Guess what Hadley's doing," Rachel said. "Guess what she's doing this very second."

I frowned. "Uh . . ."

"I'll give you a hint—it has to do with Jeremy."

Mika peered past me into the classroom. I followed her gaze and saw Hadley stuff something in Jeremy's desk.

"She's giving him a note?" I said.

"Bingo!" Rachel said. "Give the little lady a prize!"

I smiled uncertainly.

"To pay him back for how he treated you," she said. "A taste of his own medicine, you know?"

A gut-tightening worry shot through my pleasure. "What does it say?"

"Just stuff," Rachel said.

Mika laughed.

"Like what?" I said.

"Like how cute you think he is. Stuff like that."

"What?!"

"It'll mess with his mind. It'll be great."

I felt light-headed in an awful, I'm-going-to-be-sick kind of way. I tried not to show it. "Ha ha," I said. "But he'll know it's a joke. I mean, he'll know you're just fooling around."

"Alli. Darling. You are so cute," Rachel said. "Why would he think we had anything to do with it?"

And then came the part of the plan that made my knees go weak. It was *my* name they signed on the note!!!

Same day, still in social studies

Jeremy won't stop grinning at me. He read the note, I saw him, and now he won't stop grinning. I tried shaking my head at him, grimacing to indicate no, it wasn't me, and HE WINKED!

Part of me is mad at Rachel and Hadley and Mika, because they shouldn't have signed *my* name on *their* stupid note. And part of me is mad at *me*, because I should be even madder at them than I am. Mad enough to get pissed off and call them on it, because what they did wasn't nice, even if it *was* a joke. But I know I won't, because I'm a wimp. And because I don't want to mess up whatever chance I might possibly have with them.

Oh, this is ridiculous. If I were going to write a note to anyone—which I'm not—it would be to Aaron Sarmiento, not Jeremy. I don't want to be *mean* to Jeremy, but I don't want to send him love notes, either.

PLEASE LET HIM STOP GRINNING AT ME!

Same day, still in social studies
(Will this period never end?!!)

Okay. Well. This is lovely, isn't it? Jeremy stopped grinning—but only because Mr. Shakley confiscated the note!!!

Jeremy, waving the note: "Gee, Alli, thanks."
Me: "No, listen, I didn't—"

Hadley, stomping on my toes: "She didn't write it for you to share with the whole class! Right, Alli?"

Jeremy: "I'm touched, that's all I'm saying." (Poignant gaze, with hand on heart.) "I didn't know you cared."

Mr. Shakley: "What's going on back there? Jeremy, do you have a problem?"

Jeremy: "No problem."

Mr. Shakley, spotting the note: "Give it to me, Webster."

Jeremy: "It's none of your business."

Mr. Shakley: "It's my business when it happens in my class. Now give me the note, or I'll have to call your father. Again. Is that what you want?"

Jeremy: "Man!"

Mr. Shakley: ????

Jeremy, thrusting out the note: "Fine, take it!"

So then Mr. Shakley read it, while I sank as low as I could in my seat.

"Allison, see me after class," he said. "And don't let me catch you passing any more notes, or I'll be calling your parents as well. Is that understood?"

"Yes, sir," I whispered.

"Fine. Then let's get back to work." He wadded the note and threw it into the trash.

Beside me, Hadley was beet red from her efforts to stay quiet. Rachel was laughing, too, although she tried to stop when her eyes met mine. She shrugged helplessly and mouthed, "Sorry!"

Same day, English

The note is mine. It's in my backpack. I hung my head as Mr. Shakley lectured me, and when he left for hall duty, I reached into the trash can and snatched it. I am NOT uncrumpling it now, because Ms. Catrell has eagle eyes, and the last thing I need is another dose of public humiliation.

Same day, at home at last

I would have read the note as soon as I got here, but I couldn't, because Mom greeted me at the door with a plate of warm brownies.

"What are you doing here?" I asked. "Why aren't you at work?"

"Well, hello to you, too," she said. "Things were slow, so I gave everyone the afternoon off. And since I had the time, I did the good-mom thing and made some brownies. Come have one."

I followed her reluctantly to the kitchen. Why did she have to do the good-mom thing today, when I had a crisis to deal with? I picked the smallest brownie from the plate and nibbled at the corner.

"Too dry?" Mom asked.

"No, it's good."

She smiled, and I pulled myself out of my head long enough to notice how pretty she looked. So put-together looking, even though she'd changed from her work clothes into khakis and a soft cotton shirt. It was hard to imagine her ever being my age.

"Hey, Mom?" I said.

"Yes?"

"When you were in seventh grade . . . were you popular?"

She laughed.

"What?" I said.

"Allison, when I was in the seventh grade, I was a humongous dork. I wanted to be bubbly and friendly and all those things, but I was too shy. So no, I wouldn't say I was popular."

"But you wanted to be?"

"Of course. I wanted to be Rita Willis, because she was adorable and everyone drooled over her." She took a bite of brownie. "Her teeth were the tiniest bit crooked, I remember. They made her lip poke out so that it looked like she was pouting."

I experimented with my tongue, trying to make my upper lip stick out. I stopped when I realized Mom was watching. "So what did you do?"

"What do you mean?"

"You know. About wanting to be popular."

"Well, nothing, sadly enough. I read a lot. I practiced my flute." She paused. "Why? Are things not going well with you and Kathy and Megan?"

"Oh, no, everything's fine."

Mom set down her brownie. "Rita Willis," she mused. "We ended up becoming friends, but not until we were seniors. Anyway, it's funny—she told me she was never very happy in middle school. She felt like no one really knew who she was."

"She couldn't have been *that* unhappy. Everyone thought she was adorable. You said so."

"But if that's all people know you as . . ." Mom tilted her head. "Wouldn't you hate it if you had to be adorable all the time?"

"No. And I wouldn't hate people drooling over me, either."

"Hmm. Maybe not."

The phone rang, and I jumped up to get it.

"Hello?" I said.

"Alli? Hey, this is Rachel."

My heart started hammering. I walked with the phone to the far end of the kitchen and said, "Hi! What's up?"

"I was calling to see if you could spend the night this Saturday," she said, easy as pie. "It'll be you, Mika, and Hadley."

My fingers tightened on the receiver. "You want me to spend the night? At your house?"

"Well, not at a hotel. Of course at my house, you goof."

"Oh. Right. Hold on, let me check."

I pressed the phone against my chest. *Idiot, idiot, idiot,* I told myself. "Hey, Mom," I said, "is it okay if I spend the night at Rachel's this Saturday?"

"Rachel who?" Mom asked.

"Rachel Delaney."

Mom raised her eyebrows. "Rachel *Delaney?* I didn't know you two were friends."

"So can I?"

"In second grade she put—what was it? I remember. It was called Slime, and it came in a miniature garbage can. She poured it down your turtleneck."

"Mo-o-m!"

"It was that white turtleneck with the blue whales all over it. We ended up having to throw it away." She took in my pained expression. "Yes, you can spend the night. Find out where she lives and what time I should drop you off."

I relayed the questions to Rachel. My chest felt trembly as I copied down her address.

"Great," Rachel said. "I've still got to call Hadley and Mika, so I better get off the phone. Oh, but I wanted to say sorry again about what happened in social studies. Did Shakley ream you?"

I glanced at Mom and lowered my voice. "He just gave me a warning."

"Thank God," Rachel said. "So, see you tomorrow?"

"Okay. Bye."

We hung up, and I stood there, stunned, by the phone. In fact, I'm still stunned. Rachel Delaney asked me to spend the night. Not only that, but she called me before she called Mika and Hadley.

I feel like I might burst with happiness, but I'm scared, too. Because maybe I'm finally getting what I want.

Same day, two minutes later

The note. The note! Here's what it said:

> Dear Jeremy,
> I think you were very funny in class the other day. You know, with the teddy bear? Seriously, you could be a stand-up comedian.
> Anyway, that's all I wanted to tell you.
> Hugs and kisses,
> Alli
> P.S. I love that Harley-Davidson shirt you have. It's so sexy!

It's totally humiliating. I admit it. *It's so sexy?* Please!!!

I really wish they hadn't written it, but what can I do? Being pissed wouldn't change anything at this point. (Although my face is on fire imagining what Jeremy must have thought, despite the fact that I'm alone in my room.)

God. No wonder he was grinning.

Same night, 7:30 P.M.

Mika just called to make sure I'd been invited to Rachel's sleepover. I told her yes, I had, and I didn't even add, *As a matter of fact, she called me* first.

I did, however, ask her something I've been wondering about. It was a one-time-only kind of question, and I'm not entirely sure where I found the courage to ask at all. Maybe because of the fact that Rachel *had* called me first. Maybe I was still flying high from that.

What I asked Mika was this: Why was Rachel being so nice to me?

"What do you mean?" Mika said.

"I don't know," I said. "Just that . . . well, talking to me in social studies is one thing. Or even over at your house when she and Hadley came over. I happened to be there, that's all. It wasn't like she could ignore me. But this slumber party thingie . . . she actually invited me on purpose. You know?"

"Yeah, because she likes you," Mika said.

"But *why?*" I persisted.

"What do you mean, why?" Mika said. "Alli, you're being silly."

Now I felt dumb, but I wasn't quite ready to give up. "But she's . . . you know. She's *Rachel*. And I'm just me. There's nothing special about me at all."

Mika was stumped. At least that's what I assumed from her silence. And the longer it went on, the more I wished I hadn't brought this up at all.

Then Mika said, "Alli, listen. Rachel's really sure of herself, right?"

That was an understatement. Rachel was the most confident person I'd ever met.

"Um, yeah," I said.

"Well, that means she can be friends with whoever she wants. She can, like, spread the wealth, if that makes any sense. So if she likes someone, there's no reason *not* to be nice to her. Just as long as—"

"As long as what?" I said.

She hesitated, then said, "Just as long as that person is nice to her right back. That's all."

"Well, sure," I said. "Of course."

Because who wouldn't want to be nice to Rachel?

Wednesday, September 27, 4:24 P.M.

Today I ate lunch with Rachel, Mika, and Hadley, and we talked about our plans for Saturday night. (I'm so excited!) But it was my first time sitting at their table, and it was a little weird because I felt like I was on display. Like people were checking me out and saying, "Why is *she* hanging out with them? What makes her so special?" What made it worse was knowing that

Kathy and Megan were five tables away, watching my every move. I told them that Mika and I had to talk about our history paper, and that was the only reason I was sitting there. I don't think they believed me.

But I had fun, even though I was too nervous to actually eat my pizza. Rachel, Mika, and Hadley all scribbled their e-mail addresses in my math notebook, and when I got home, I sent a message to Rachel first thing. Here's what I wrote:

Hey, Rachel. What's up? (Other than the sky, that is. Ha ha. My dad says that all the time, and it is sooooo corny.) Right now I'm eating a bagel with cream cheese, with crushed up Doritos smushed all over it. It sounds gross, but it tastes awesome. You should try it!

Then I paused, thinking about how to put the next part. I'd wanted to bring it up at lunch—turns out I couldn't let go of it after all—but my mouth got dry every time I tried. Finally I started typing.

So you know that note to Jeremy? (Duh. Of course you do.) I was wondering, why did you guys sign MY name to it? I'm not mad or anything. I'm just curious. But it's no big deal.
Okay, well, back to my bagel. Bye!!!

I hit the SEND button before I could chicken out. Then I fooled around on the Net for a while. I was hoping Rachel would respond before I logged off, and she did. My pulse sped up as I clicked on OPEN. Here's what she said:

> *Alli-cat! The only reason we put your name on the note is because it seemed more believable that way. (Don't worry, we don't think you actually like him or anything. As if!) You don't mind, do you? Write back and tell me, because now I'm all worried!!!*
>
> *Later, gator.*
> *Rachel*
> *P.S. Doritos and cream cheese? Ewww!*

I quickly typed my response.

> No, no, I totally don't mind. It was just the part about his shirt that kinda bugged me, about how sexy it is. You know?

I gnawed on my thumbnail, then sent the message. And then I wished I hadn't, because I didn't want her to think I'm the type of person who gets uptight about things like that. I guess it's okay, though, because her next message was really sweet.

> *Oh my God, I SO don't blame you. I told Hadley not to put that part, but she did anyway. You are such a good sport for not freaking out. (Do you know what Hadley would do if someone told Jeremy that SHE thought he was sexy? She'd fly into a rage and break things. I'm not kidding!!!)*

No more notes to Jeremy. I promise.
Tootles!

I'm glad that she apologized (well, sort of apologized), and it makes me feel good that she thinks I handled the whole thing better than Hadley would have. But at the same time, her comment about the note being more believable coming from me is perhaps not the most flattering thing that could be said.

Then again, it's probably true. Rachel wouldn't send a note like that to Jeremy in a million years, and neither would Hadley or Mika.

Then again, neither would I.

Same day, 5:05 p.m.

Oh, well. I'll steer clear of Jeremy from now on, and he'll figure out the truth soon enough.

Only three more days until the sleepover!!!

Thursday, September 28, study hall

I can't believe it. According to Kathy, I'm a wannabe. She told me this at lunch, which is very funny since if I *were* a wannabe, I'd have been sitting at the cool table with Rachel, Mika, and Hadley instead of with Kathy and Megan, who I *thought* were my friends. But now they're acting like jerks just because I can't spend every single minute with them.

Yes, I have to go to Mika's this afternoon to work on our project. Big deal. Kathy and Megan have been working on their project every day this week, and you don't hear me complaining. And, okay, I can't spend the night at Megan's on Saturday because I happen to have other plans, and those plans happen to be with Rachel. So shoot me! I'm not allowed to have other friends?

It was bad, how it all came out. I'd been eating my meat loaf and half listening to Kathy and Megan, who were talking about some TV show I haven't even heard of. Kathy wants to get her hair cut like one of the characters, and Megan kept teasing her about Jared and neck tickles and no more scrunchies, whatever that means. For someone who doesn't really want to be friends with Kathy, Megan sure was doing a good job of faking it. Anyway, they giggled away like crazy giggling people, and I wondered when they'd formed so many inside jokes without me.

"Have you seen it?" Megan asked me, referring to the show.

I shook my head. "Mika and I have been working superhard on our project, so I really don't have time for TV."

"Or anything else," Kathy said under her breath.

"What?" I said.

"But not today, right?" Kathy went on. "Today you're going with us to Curiosities. I want to buy those earrings if they're still on sale." My face must have given me away, because she put down her fork. "Alli! You better not say you forgot!"

"I'm sorry!" I said. "Mika called right before I went to bed, and I completely spaced that we were supposed to go shopping. And we *do* have to finish our paper. The History Fair's only a week away!"

"Oh, please," Kathy said.

Megan jumped in and said, "Hey, I know. We could go shopping on Saturday if you guys want. Mom said you could both spend the night at our new place, kind of like a housewarming party."

Kathy pursed her lips. "Well, I guess that would be okay. Alli?"

"Uh . . . could we do it on Friday instead?"

Megan shook her head. "Mom said it'll be too hectic, because that'll be our first night there. Saturday's better."

"Do you have a problem with that?" Kathy asked.

They looked at me.

I shoved my chair away from the table. "I can't do it on Saturday. Sorry." I picked up my tray and headed for the back of the cafeteria.

Kathy scrambled out of her seat. "What's wrong with Saturday?"

"I have other plans."

"*What* other plans?"

My stomach tightened, but I said, "Kathy, come on. It's not like you and Megan are the only people I can hang out with."

She stopped in her tracks. I kept walking, and when I returned from putting up my tray, she was still standing there. Her cheeks were red. That's when she called me a wannabe.

"You care more about Mika and Rachel than you do about us!" she said. "You'd rather be *popular* than be with your real friends!"

She said it like it was a disease. Like it was this huge sin to want people to like you, when I knew she was just jealous. Otherwise, why would she care?

I returned to our table to grab my backpack.

"Alli's not coming on Saturday," Kathy announced. "She's ditching us for Rachel Delaney."

"I'm not . . ." I tried to swallow. "It's just this one Saturday. And if you had invited me earlier . . ."

Megan gazed at me, her expression more hurt than mad. I got my stuff and turned to leave.

"Alli!" Kathy cried. "You can't just—"

"Let her go," I heard Megan say.

My heart beat fast and hard. Which is totally unfair, because I didn't do anything wrong.

Friday, September 29, homeroom

I made a point of finding Kathy this morning and acting completely normal, complaining about my math homework and how evil Mr. Schuler is. But did she act normal back? *Nooooooo.* I complimented her earrings, the ones she got at Curiosities, and she said, "Well, thanks, but I hope you don't think that changes things."

Megan came up while we were talking, and even she acted a little sketchy. Like, she smiled when I told her I liked her BOLDER BOULDER shirt, but not in a way that reached her eyes.

Same night, 8:28 P.M.

I IM-ed Kathy after dinner, but all I got was her stupid autoresponse, which was insanely annoying because her name was on my buddy list. So our conversation, if you can call it that, went like this:

alli-cat12: hiya, kath. wazzup?

Auto response from MizKitty: smells like teen spirit!

alli-cat12: kathy, c'mon. i KNOW you're there.

alli-cat12: fine, be that way. but i don't know why u refuse to consider the possibility that rachel and mika and hadley might be perfectly nice, WHICH THEY ARE. just because i happen to like them doesn't make me a bad person. anyway, ur the one who first got all chummy with megan, remember? but u didn't hear ME complaining. i said, "great, cool, let's all be buds," because that's what friends do. so if anyone's acting snobby here, it's U!!!!

And then I screwed up my courage and hit SEND. So there!

Same night, 9:15 P.M.

Kathy hasn't called *or* IM-ed *or* e-mailed. She's acting extremely juvenile.

I did get an IM from Megan, though. Here's our convo:

megawatt: hey, alli. wazzup?

alli-cat12: megan! HI! wazzup with u?

megawatt: not much. i just wanted to say sorry for being weird today.

alli-cat12: oh

megawatt: yeah. i've been thinking about it, and i'm like, "so she has plans on saturday nite. big deal." right? i mean, it's not like u could change them just for me.

alli-cat12: i already said yes to rachel, that's all. other-
     wise i totally would.
megawatt: i know. i'm just bummed.
megawatt: it's just, i kinda feel like u've dumped me on
     kathy, that's all. like, it started out being the 3 of us,
     and now it's just me and her.

I paused. At first I'd been glad she'd IM-ed, but now I felt a
little annoyed. Because sure, she was IM-ing to apologize, but
really she just wanted to guilt-trip me some more.

alli-cat12: u guys'll have a blast. just like at lunch, when
     u were laffing about that tv show or whatever.
alli-cat12: to tell the truth, i was sorta surprised.
     i was like, "huh. guess they've gotten really
     close."
megawatt: just cuz we were laffing doesn't mean we've
     gotten close. altho at least kathy's willing to do stuff
     with me.

And then for a minute the screen stayed blank, because she
wasn't typing anything, and I sure wasn't either. Because it
made me mad that she would act like I wasn't doing stuff with
her on purpose. Like I was *choosing* not to spend time with her.
Finally, I placed my hands back over the keys.

alli-cat12: this is dumb, megan.
megawatt: i know. i'm sorry.

alli-cat12: listen. get your room set up this weekend, and i'll come over very soon and see it, ok?

megawatt: promise?

alli-cat12: i promise. and having kathy there won't be so bad, cuz she's actually pretty good with decorating. like, she always reads those "seventeen" articles about making curtains out of bedsheets and stuff.

megawatt: if u say so

alli-cat12: i do. it'll be fun.

And then we chatted a little while longer about regular stuff, and it wasn't great, but it wasn't terrible. Now if only Kathy would call, everything would go back to normal. Except for one thing: I'm no longer sure what "normal" is.

Same day, 11:02 P.M.

Kathy's not going to call. Her parents would kill her if she used the phone after eleven, and so would mine.

So I decided to stop worrying about it and put on a nose strip, which I needed to do anyway in preparation for tomorrow. Its deep-cleansing action is kicking in. I can feel it. The only problem is that fifteen minutes suddenly seems like a long time to wait, because I am SO sleepy. But if I peel it off now, then who knows how much gunk will be left in my pores, and I'll be hardly better off than I was before.

Saturday, September 30, 9:22 A.M.

Oh. My. God. I am deformed.

I am deformed, and Rachel, Mika, and Hadley will gasp in

horror and call me Nostril Girl. DAMN THOSE STUPID NOSE STRIPS!!!

I fell asleep with the one from last night still on, and by this morning it had hardened into concrete. I am so not kidding. I had to use Mom's rubbing alcohol to get it off, and even then it left blobs of glue which clung to my nose. I had to pick at them one by one, and most of them came off okay, except for a bit on my left nostril that peeled away a layer of skin and left a red sore.

I tried covering it up with some of Mom's foundation, but it stung too much, and anyway it didn't work. I can still see the rawness beneath.

I look like a leper.

Why do these things always happen to ME?!!!

Same day, Rachel's bathroom

My nose and I have arrived. No one has commented on the red spot—yet. One reason may be that I've spent a fair amount of time here in the bathroom, both to check on my nostril and to give myself occasional breaks from the sleepover madness. I'm having a great time, don't get me wrong, but it's taking its toll. Like, I've been trying so hard to be cool that my brain feels stretched out. Also, I've been experimenting with a more sophisticated smile, which I practiced last night before I conked out. My cheek muscles ache.

I just realized that all this probably sounds pathetic, as if I'm a total poser freak who'll do anything to impress Rachel and Hadley and Mika. But that's not it at all. I'm just being the me I want to be, even if it takes a little extra effort.

Hmm. It is true, however, that being me is a lot easier when I'm with Kathy and Megan. (At least, that used to be true.) It's also true that when I first got here, my gut instinct was to turn and run and never come back. But that's because just stepping inside Rachel's house totally freaked me out.

"Wow," I said. My eyes traveled to the high ceilings of the entry hall. "You live in a mansion."

"Hardly," Rachel said. "Although it was built by the same architect who built the Swan Coach House."

"For real? Wow." I had no clue what the Swan Coach House was. I walked over to a grandfather clock that was taller than me. In an open panel above the face, a yellow moon inched across the night sky.

"It's an antique," Rachel informed me. She gestured to her left. "So is that dresser. My mom loves antiques. They're the only furniture she'll buy."

Mom loves antiques, too, but ours come from garage sales.

Rachel grabbed my bag and headed for the staircase. "Come on, Mika and Hadley are already here. And let me warn you, Hadley's being a pain. So just ignore her, okay?"

Upstairs, we followed a long hall and turned left into Rachel's bedroom, which, like the rest of the house, was immense.

"Alli, hey," Mika said. She smiled and put down her magazine.

"Hi," I said. I glanced at Hadley, who sat on the floor with her arms around a giant, stuffed panda. "Hi, Hadley."

Hadley didn't respond.

"Aren't you going to say hello?" Rachel demanded.

Hadley dug her chin into the top of the panda.

"That is so rude," Rachel said. To me, she added, "I can't believe how rude she's being. I am so sorry."

"That's okay," I said.

Rachel flopped down on her bed. "She's mad because I wouldn't go to Papa Murphy's with her."

"I am not," Hadley muttered.

"She has a crush on a guy who works there," Mika explained.

"I do *not!*"

"Oh, please," Rachel said. "Everybody knows, so stop being such a drama queen." She turned to me. "She wanted me to go in with her so she could flirt with him, only she never does flirt with him. She always chickens out."

Hadley got up and stomped to the bathroom.

Mika gnawed on her thumbnail. "You want me to go talk to her?"

"Why? You know what she's going to say. Anyway, that guy at Papa Murphy's isn't even cute. Hadley's, like, oversexed. That's what my mom says."

I wrapped my arms around my chest.

Mika stared at the rug.

Rachel looked from me to Mika and said, "Crap. Now you guys hate me, don't you?"

"We don't hate you," Mika said.

"Well, you should. I didn't mean that about Hadley."

"I know," Mika said.

"I really didn't, Alli."

I hesitated, then said, "Friends sometimes get mad at each

other, and it's no one's fault. People shouldn't, you know, get all worked up about it."

Rachel nodded. It made me feel good, the way she was looking at me. "Yeah. You are so right."

She hopped off the bed. "Hey, I know what let's do. My dad bought my mom a copy of *Playgirl* for a joke. Let's go find it." She raised her voice. "We're going to my parents' room, Hadley."

Rachel talked over her shoulder as we headed down the hall. "He bought it for her birthday—talk about oversexed, huh? Plus he has a whole stash of *Playboys* in the back of his closet. We can look at them, too."

A familiar nervousness balled up inside me. I had never even seen a *Playboy* before, much less a *Playgirl*. My parents don't buy magazines like that, I'm pretty positive. (And if they did, I sure wouldn't tell my friends!)

We went in her parents' bedroom and shut the door. Rachel opened the bottom drawer of her mom's bedside cabinet. "If she still has it, this is where it'll be."

Mika grabbed my sleeve. "I can't believe we're doing this!"

My mouth was dry. But when Rachel said, "Hey, check this out!" and pulled out a roll of condoms, a nervous giggle squeaked out.

"Your mom uses *condoms?*" Mika said.

"No, but I have a feeling my dad does," Rachel said.

"You know what I mean. Yuck, I wonder what my parents use!"

I don't want to know what my parents use. I don't even want to know if they have sex.

"Ha! Here it is!" Rachel cried, pulling the *Playgirl* from under a stack of *Ladies' Home Journal*s. She opened it to the centerfold. "Look."

Mika and I crowded around her. I took a quick peek, saw nothing but a lot of hair, then forced myself to look again. I gulped.

"Is it real?" Mika whispered.

"Well, yeah," Rachel said. "What do you think, it's like an artificial limb or something?"

I leaned in, peering over Mika's shoulder.

Someone opened the door, and the three of us shrieked.

"It's just me," Hadley said. "Geez!" She looked as if she'd been crying, but that could have been my imagination.

Rachel put her hand over her heart. "You scared the piss out of me. Ever heard of knocking?"

"What are you guys doing?" Hadley asked.

Rachel considered. Then she stepped back from the bed and said, "Check it out."

Hadley came forward. She spotted the centerfold, and her eyebrows shot up. "Holy crapola."

The rest of us cracked up.

"Hey," Rachel said in a low voice. "Honey-roasted penis."

"Huh?" I said.

Hadley met Rachel's eyes. "Honey-roasted penis," she repeated in a voice a little louder than Rachel's.

"Oh God," Mika said. "Honey-roasted penis!" She covered her face.

Hadley nudged me with her elbow. "Your turn. You have to say it even louder."

My heart pounded. "I do?"

"Uh-huh."

I glanced at the door, which was cracked open from when Hadley came in. Rachel's parents were out there somewhere, probably having a martini or a scotch or some other ritzy drink. I turned to Mika, but she was no help. She watched me through her fingers and dissolved into giggles.

"Uh, honey-roasted peanuts?" I said.

Rachel formed an *X* with her fingers and buzzed me out.

I took a breath. Everyone was waiting. "Honey-roasted penis!"

Rachel slapped me a high five. "Honey-roasted PENIS!" she crowed.

"HONEY-ROASTED *PENIS!!!*" yelled Hadley.

"Girls! What in the world is going on?" Rachel's mom demanded. She stared at us from the doorway.

"Mom! Hi!" Rachel said. She sat down on the bed, on top of the open *Playgirl*. "Were we being too loud?"

"I can hear you from downstairs. So can your father." She frowned. "And why honey-roasted peanuts? I thought you girls were saving room for Chinese."

We lost it, all four of us. Mika snorted and fell against me, while Hadley turned practically purple.

"We are," Rachel said. "We'll be right there."

And that's where they are now, pigging out on Kung Pao chicken and Diet Coke. I better get down there before they think I fell into the toilet. Anyway, I need to eat so I'll have strength for the rest of the night. Otherwise I'll never be able to keep up.

Same night, in the hall outside Rachel's room

The others are sleeping, I'm pretty sure. And I should be, too, only I can't, because I've made a huge mistake. BUT IT WAS AN ACCIDENT! IT REALLY, REALLY WAS!

After dinner the four of us piled on the sofa to watch *Blue Crush* on the Delaneys' wide-screen TV. It's set up with surround sound, so it's kind of like being in your own private movie theater. Anne-Marie was paddling her surfboard back into the ocean after nearly drowning, which of course was completely unbelievable. Any normal person would have given up. But we'd all seen the movie before, so we knew that the next wave she caught was going to be perfect. She would surf it like a pro in her cute little bikini bottom and Billabong shirt, and she'd end up on the cover of *Surf* magazine, all because she'd had the guts to stay true to herself. Maybe it *was* unbelievable, but it was inspiring all the same.

Anyway, we were squealing and clapping our hands and I guess being a little on the noisy side, because Rachel's dad strode into the room and turned off the TV.

"I want you girls to go upstairs *now*," he ordered. Usually you get a warning or two when a parent's had enough, but with Mr. Delaney it was like, *Bang! Get to your room this second!*

"But Dad, we're just at the good part," Rachel said, hurriedly pushing herself up so that she wasn't draped over the cushion. "We'll be quiet, I promise." She aimed the remote and pressed the power button.

Mr. Delaney barreled over, snatched the remote, and snapped the TV back off. "Do you want me to send everyone home, Rachel? Is that what you want?"

Color flooded Rachel's face. She pressed her lips together, then stood up and left the room. Mika, Hadley, and I followed in dead silence.

"I *hate* him," she said when we tried to console her. She sat on her bed with her knees to her chest. "I'm not kidding. I wish he would take that job in L.A. like he's always threatening to."

Mika and Hadley glanced at each other. Clearly this was something they'd heard before.

Hadley hitched her shoulders. "Last night, my dad yelled at me for getting a sixty-eight on my math quiz. I was like, 'Dad, come on. You should be happy I passed.'"

Rachel's expression didn't change.

"At least your dad tells you when he's mad," Mika said. "One time my dad went for two days without saying a word to any of us."

Rachel snorted. As in, *I should be so lucky.*

I felt as if it were my turn, but I didn't know what to contribute. Dad doesn't yell or give Mom and me the silent treatment. In fact, sometimes Mom gets irritated because he *won't* get angry. "For heaven's sake, Dan, can't you see I need to fight about this?" she'll say.

I couldn't tell Rachel that. It would come out like bragging. So I said the only thing that popped into my head, which was, "My friend Megan's dad is *really* bad. He, like, totally walked out on her and her mom."

"Megan Campbell?" Hadley said. "That new kid?"

Sweat pricked my armpits. I realized I'd screwed up. "Uh . . ."

"The one who wore that hideous cat shirt?" Hadley went on.

"Her grandmother gave her that shirt," I said quickly. "She

had to wear it." Maybe if we could talk about bad fashion choices, they'd forget the rest. "It *was* pretty hideous, huh?"

"Her dad walked out on her?" Rachel said. Nothing in her manner had changed, exactly, except I could sense a ripple of interest.

"That's horrible," Mika said. *"Why?"*

"It happens all the time," Hadley said. "Not here, obviously, but in slums and inner cities and stuff."

"Wow," Mika said. "Poor Megan."

"Wait," I said. "He didn't . . . I mean, he . . ." I felt panicky. "You guys can't tell *anybody*, okay? Megan would kill me."

"Of course," Mika said.

Hadley sealed her lips with her thumb and forefinger.

I guess Rachel could see that I was upset, because she reached over and rubbed my shoulder. "Don't worry. We can keep a secret."

Same night, same place

At least no one noticed my nose.

Sunday, October 1, 1:02 P.M.

I IM-ed Mika when I got home, supposedly to talk about our project but really to remind her not to say anything about Megan. Here's what she said, after we got through with the boring stuff:

alli-cat12: so, listen. u've really, really, really got to promise not to say anything about megan's dad, cuz she's extremely sensitive about it. ok?

mikasa: don't worry, i won't.

alli-cat12: i know u never would. i'm just paranoid, i guess.

mikasa: my lips are zipped. i feel awful for her, tho.

alli-cat12: i know. me 2.

alli-cat12: what about rachel and hadley? u think they'll remember not to tell?

mikasa: alli! geez, u R paranoid. no one's going to say anything, i promise.

alli-cat12: well just, u know, remind them if u get the chance. if the topic happens to come up.

I didn't want her to think I was this big needy wimp, so I changed the subject.

alli-cat12: so what was going on with rachel and hadley? when i first got there, i mean.

mikasa: oh, god. r u talking about the papa murphy's guy?

alli-cat12: i guess. why didn't rachel just go with her to see him, if hadley wanted her to so much?

mikasa: BECAUSE

alli-cat12: cuz why?

mikasa: well, now it's your turn to swear to secrecy. IF i tell u, that is.

alli-cat12: tell me—u have to!

mikasa: cuz the last time we went to papa m's, the waiter—his name's roby—had the nerve to pay attention to hadley instead of rachel.

alli-cat12: ohhh

alli-cat12: so rachel was jealous?

mikasa: usually guys fall all over themselves for her, so it's kinda like she expects it. i don't mean that in a bad way. she just gets pissy about stuff sometimes.

mikasa: actually, that's something u should probably know. she, like, gets into these moods.

alli-cat12: why is that something i should know?

mikasa: never mind. i don't know why i said that. but just remember to stay on her good side, ok?

In front of my computer, I lifted my eyebrows. It was as if a whole new Mika had opened up online, one who said all kinds of stuff she would never say in person. I felt a little guilty, like we shouldn't be talking about Rachel behind her back, but at the same time I was totally fascinated.

alli-cat12: have U ever been on her bad side?

There was a pause, and my stomach dropped. I'd gone too far. But then her answer flashed onto the screen.

mikasa: remember that play we did in mr. rubichek's class last year?

alli-cat12: no. was it during fall semester?

mikasa: oh yeah. u probably missed it. well, mr. rubichek assigned me to be the narrator, which was the part rachel wanted. i even went to mr. rubichek and tried to get him to change it, but he wouldn't.

alli-cat12: so what did rachel do?

mikasa: she thought i'd gone for the part on purpose, which totally wasn't true.

alli-cat12: so what did she DO?

mikasa: well . . . she just wasn't very nice.

alli-cat12: like how?

mikasa: it's not important. anyway, it was soooo long ago.

alli-cat12: MIKA

mikasa: no, really. all i'm saying is that usually rachel is super super nice. U know. but sometimes she's not. that's all.

mikasa: listen, i've g2g. my mom wants to go over my japanese homework.

alli-cat12: oh. ok.

mikasa: don't forget to bring our diorama tomorrow. bye!

I logged off and flopped onto my bed, where I am now. I should be doing some homework of my own, but I'm too busy thinking about what Mika said. It gave me a thrill, kind of, to get the inside scoop about Rachel not being totally perfect. I actually liked hearing it, because it was like, *Okay, now we're a little more even. Maybe our friendship's not such a stretch after all.*

Although I also felt a pang when Mika mentioned the whole play thing, since once again that was something I wasn't part of. And Mika hadn't even noticed. (Not that she should have.)

I wish I could find out what Rachel did to Mika, but the only person I could ask is Kathy, and I'm not about to do that.

But obviously it wasn't too bad, or Mika wouldn't still be her friend.

Same day, 1:35 P.M.

I wonder if Kathy and Megan had fun last night, hanging out at Megan's new place.

Monday, October 2, 4:33 P.M.

Things I Will Not Do If Kathy Wants to
Hang Out with Someone New

1. Make fake-sweet comments at the lunch table, like, "Are you really going to sit with us? *Really?!!!*"
2. Proceed to clap ecstatically and dab away tears of gladness.
3. Ask questions about her new friends, emphasizing the word *new* in a drawn-out, obnoxious way.
4. Announce a fresh code of conduct, where whenever she's confused about what to do, she could ask herself this simple question: What Would Rachel Do?
5. Write the letters WWRD on a napkin and proclaim it a handy reminder of said code.
6. Tuck the handy reminder into her backpack and make clucking sounds, exclaiming over how my little girl is growing up. If anyone needs to grow up, it's HER.

Tuesday, October 3, study hall

Another thing I will not do if Kathy becomes friends with new people: I will not stomp off in a sulk if she tells me she has to work on her history project during study hall. First of all, it IS study hall, and Kathy shouldn't have been in my classroom in the first place. And if Ms. Chadwick (or Celia, as she insists we call her) cared as much about teaching as she does about being cool, there wouldn't have been a problem. But no. Ms. Chadwick always reads *Cosmo* behind her desk, and she always lets us chat.

And second of all, despite popular opinion, I am NOT slaving away on my project because I love making dioramas of the olden days. How many times do I have to explain this? The History Fair is in three days, and I have a lot to get done. Just because Mika happens to be my partner does not change the fact that THIS IS FOR A GRADE!!!

Uh-oh, here comes Ms. Chadwick. I better get busy on something besides this journal. Then again, what am I saying? I'll just compliment her nail polish, and off we'll go on an endless chat about fashion and style.

Same day, social studies

Megan's not being so bad, I guess. Unlike Kathy. She caught up with me after fifth period—it was just the two of us—and she was like, "Alli?" With this question in her eyes.

"What?" I said. I didn't want to hear it, whatever it was, because I'd had enough guilt trips for one day. Plus, when I looked at her, I thought about what I'd told Rachel and the others. It made me afraid to be alone with her.

"Nothing," she said. "I just kind of wanted to talk to you, that's all. Because I've been feeling really—" She broke off. Frowned. "Are you wearing mascara?"

I blushed. "No."

"Are you sure?"

Of course I was sure. I'd only put on the *teeniest* amount. "I'm not wearing mascara. What did you want to talk to me about?"

"There's nothing wrong with it," Megan said. "It looks good."

I gripped the strap of my backpack. "You think I'm trying too hard, don't you? That's what you're secretly thinking."

"Huh?"

"You think it's dumb to want to look pretty."

She drew her eyebrows together. "Alli, that's not what I'm thinking at all. I swear."

I ducked my head. Stupidness rose up inside me.

Megan touched my shoulder. "If you want to wear makeup, you can. You can do whatever you want to do."

And then it was time for social studies. And I had to go.

Same day, still in social studies

I'm pretty sure Rachel noticed my mascara, too, because when I sat down at the beginning of class, she smiled and said, "Hey, Alli. You look really good."

It made me feel embarrassed, like I must have put on way more than I meant to, but not as embarrassed as when Megan said something. Because Rachel wears tons of makeup already. Not in a bad way, but it's definitely there.

Same day, after social studies

Oh good God. *Jeremy.* All during class, he sat hunched over his desk crumpling teeny little balls of paper out of the wiggly bits sticking out of his spiral. Just normal waste-of-time Jeremy, right? But on the way out of class he came up behind me and dumped the whole lot of them over my head.

I blushed, and Jeremy about split a gut.

"Nice," Rachel said. "Now they're all in her hair."

"Nuh-uh, it's dandruff," Jeremy said.

I shook my head, and bits of paper showered down. Rachel plucked at the ones I couldn't get.

"Admit it, it was funny," he wheedled.

"Hysterical," Rachel said. "You should go on the road."

"I probably will. When I'm older, that's probably what I'll do."

Rachel stopped picking. She looked at him dead-on. "I mean right now. What are you waiting for?"

His smile wavered.

"Go on, leave," she said.

He hesitated, then laughed again. He loped off down the hall.

"Loser," she said under her breath. She gazed at me. "You can't let him treat you that way, Alli."

"I know," I whispered.

"What?"

"I said I know."

She raised her eyebrows as if she didn't believe me. She stepped closer and brushed the remaining scraps off my shoulder. "There. Good as new."

Wednesday, October 4, 7:15 P.M.

Well, I just got off the phone with Kathy. We didn't eat lunch together today, and I didn't see her before math like I sometimes do, so when Mom yelled that Kathy was on the line, my heart leaped in a glad kind of way. Although the very next second my palms got sweaty, which was strange.

As I jogged downstairs, I readied my casual tone, as if nothing screwy was going on between us. But Kathy jumped in as soon as I said hi, and the speech she gave me wasn't casual at all. It was about how friends should be there for each other no matter what, especially in times of trouble. (Her words, not mine.) The speech went on for a long time, and what it boiled down to was that Megan's dad, who was supposed to come for a visit this weekend, is no longer coming.

My stomach dropped when she told me. "Crap," I said.

"Uh-huh," Kathy said in this accusing way, as if *I* were the one who'd blown Megan off. "Megan's really upset."

I sat down on the kitchen floor. "Did he say why?"

"He's got a golf game with some hotshot manager guy at his company. Apparently it's more important than seeing his daughter."

"A golf game?"

"And she and her mom have been working so hard on their new house, trying to get it all fixed up before he got here." She paused. "It looks fabulous, not that you would know."

I felt kind of sick. This must have been what Megan wanted to talk about yesterday, when somehow the conversation got sidetracked.

"I just really think you should call her," Kathy said. "She could use a friend right now."

I closed my eyes and nodded.

"Alli?" Kathy said.

"I will, as soon as I get off with you."

Same night, 8:46 P.M.

I hate Megan's dad! Even though I've never met him, I hate him. What kind of father would promise to visit and then *cancel* it, just like that?

When I called her, Megan told me she doesn't know if he's going to drive down some other time or not. And she doesn't know how Fred's doing, because she didn't ask. She said she pretty much stopped wanting to talk after he announced he wasn't coming, which I completely understand.

"Did you ask if maybe he could maybe reschedule his game?" I asked.

"He said it was important for him to be there," she said.

"Well, did you, you know, argue with him? Not *argue*. But tell him that it was important to you, too?"

She was silent.

"He told me he didn't have time to talk to me if all I was going to do was sulk," she said at last.

"Oh, Megan."

"It was a total shutdown remark. And it worked."

"Yuck." I wanted to say so much more, but I didn't know how. Talking about her dad at all felt like dangerous ground.

"I didn't tell Kathy," she said. "I mean, I told her my dad wasn't coming, but I didn't tell her . . . that part."

"That's okay," I said. Which was dumb, because it's not as if I needed to give her permission. I meant it more as in, *Your*

dad's being awful, and I'm sorry, and you don't have to tell anyone you don't want to.

"Yeah," she said. "And then, you know, I almost didn't even tell you. I *wanted* to, but . . ."

My fingers tightened on the phone. "I know."

"You've been pretty busy lately."

"I know," I said again. Quickly.

"I don't want to bug you with my problems."

"*Megan.*"

More silence. The den, where I was sitting, had gotten dark as twilight came on, and I was glad because it meant no one could see me. Not that there was anyone *to* see me, but still.

I took a breath. "Just because I sometimes hang out with other people, that doesn't change things between you and me."

Now it was her turn to say, "I know."

"Really, Megan. I'm telling the truth."

She sighed a big long sigh. It kind of cleared the air.

"Thanks, Alli."

I watched the shadows stretch across the floor. "Anytime."

Friday, October 6, 6:44 P.M.

Tonight is the night of the History Fair! Wh-hoo! As soon as Dad finds his car keys, the two of us are heading to the school. I'm actually a little nervous, which is silly. It's not like we're going to the Academy Awards. But everyone will be there, and not just the seventh graders but the eighth graders, too. Eighth graders always make me nervous.

Mom was supposed to come with us, but at the last minute she got a call from her office. Somebody accidentally erased the placement test results from some file, and Mom had to go try to fix things. At first I was bummed—the History Fair only lasts one night—but then I thought, *Yes. The miniskirt.* Rachel brought it to school today for me to borrow, but when Mom saw me in it, she had a cow.

"Allison, that is far too short," she said.

"Mom," I complained.

"Sorry, babe, but no. How about that patchwork skirt Aunt Suzy gave you?"

The patchwork skirt Aunt Suzy gave me comes to my ankles, practically, and just because our project's about the Pilgrims doesn't mean I have to dress like one.

So I waited until Mom left and then changed back into Rachel's miniskirt. I wonder what Rachel'll say when she sees me in it. I wonder what Kathy and Megan will say.

Yikes—Dad's calling. Got to go!

Same night, 9:10 P.M.

Whew. I had to sprint to my room the minute Dad and I got home, because Mom pulled into the driveway right behind us, and I didn't want her noticing my outfit. But now I'm in my *Too Sweet to Eat* pj's with the cherries and strawberries and orange slices all over them. In a minute I'll go back downstairs and tell Mom all about the night.

But first I've got to write down my huge, exciting news. RACHEL IS HAVING A PARTY!!! Her birthday's next Friday, and she's inviting a ton of kids over to her house to celebrate. Girls *and* boys. There may even be a few eighth graders. (Help!) But it's going to be great, I just know it. And it's only a week away!

So here's what happened. Dad and I got to school at around 7:10, and I could see from all the cars that lots of people were already there.

"Hold on," I said when Dad came around to my side. I tugged at the hem of Rachel's skirt. "Do I look all right?"

"You look beautiful," he said. Only he always says that, so I can never really believe him.

We walked into the auditorium, and Mika ran up to us first thing.

"Omigod, you look fabulous," she said to me.

"Really?" I said. "You don't think it's too short?"

She grabbed my arm. "Come on, we've got to find Rachel and Hadley." She dragged me across the room to one of the refreshment tables, where Rachel lifted her Coke in greeting.

"Alli!" she said. She took in my skirt. "It fits—that's awesome. Do you like it?"

"I love it," I said.

"Keep it as long as you want. Hadley was thinking about wearing it to the party, but it looks better on you than it does on her." She turned to Hadley. "You don't care, do you, Hadley?"

I took in Hadley's expression. Then I shifted back to Rachel. "Uh . . . what party?"

Rachel grinned. She told me about her birthday party while Mika nodded beside her.

"It's going to be a blast," Rachel said. She reeled off the names of the people she planned to invite, including guys like Carter Hunt and Tyler Adams, who were the most popular guys in the grade. She listed Aaron Sarmiento's name, too. My stomach dipped just hearing it.

"Oh, and Jeremy Webster, of course," Rachel said. "We can't forget Jeremy."

I followed Rachel's gaze across the room to where Jeremy was prying Popsicle sticks off someone's miniature log cabin. "Ha ha," I said, to show I knew she was joking. As if Rachel would ever invite Jeremy.

Rachel laughed.

"But tell her the rest," Mika said. "About how we can invite people, too, if there's anyone special we want to ask."

"Totally," Rachel said. "Like if you want to invite Kathy and Megan, Alli, that's fine by me."

"Seriously?"

"Sure, as long as they worship me for the goddess I am."

I blinked, and she lifted one eyebrow to show that once again she was kidding. About the worshiping part this time, not the invite.

I glanced at Megan and Kathy's "First Thanksgiving" display, which was several tables away. Megan was rearranging one of the cornucopias, and beside her stood Kathy, wearing a red top I'd never seen. Excitement danced inside me, and I wanted to rush over and invite them right then. I knew I should wait, though. So I did.

"What food are you going to serve?" Mika asked.

"I haven't completely decided," Rachel said. "What do you think?"

I half listened as they discussed chips and dip, Hovan rolls, and twenty-foot subs. But mainly I thought how great it would be if we could *all* end up being friends—Rachel and Mika and Hadley *plus* Megan and Kathy. Then I wouldn't have to worry about picking one group over the other.

"Hey," I said, focusing back in. "My mom makes really yummy brownies. Want me to get her to bake a batch?"

"Sure," Rachel said. "You can bring them over early, when we're getting everything set up. And M&M's, we definitely need M&M's."

"Especially the green ones," Hadley said.

Everyone giggled, me included. We are going to have so much fun.

Same night, 10:45 P.M.

Must go to bed. Must! But I can't, because my brain is whizzing along at a hundred miles an hour.

I just got back upstairs from telling Mom about the fair. I showed her our diorama, and she told me she was really proud. And I don't think she was faking, because she noticed all of the special details like the teeny tiny blades of grass, which she said showed "impressive workmanship."

"Thanks," I said. "Mika did the tepee, and I did Pocahontas and all the animals."

"The animals are my favorite part," Mom said. "You've definitely got talent, Allison."

I got warm when she said that. I had wondered if it was as good as I thought it was.

"Guess who else admired your project?" Dad asked.

"Who?"

"Kathy and Megan and Megan's mother," he said. "Kathy said it should have won first place instead of the Civil War costume."

"She did?"

"She did."

Huh, I thought. "What about Megan? Did she say anything?"

"Megan liked it, too. She was the one who pointed out the deer."

I'd worked really hard on that deer. I didn't want it to look all plastic-y and dumb.

"I think they miss you," he said, totally out of the blue.

"What?!" I said. I shook my head. "Dad, you think you know everything about kids because you're a teacher. Kathy and Megan don't *miss* me. If they missed me, they would have come and found me. They do have feet, you know."

"Sometimes it's hard when one person in a group decides to branch out," Dad said.

For some reason that made my muscles tighten. "Anyway, we're all hanging out together next Friday," I said. "Rachel's having a birthday party, and Kathy and Megan are coming."

"Really?" Mom said. She seemed surprised, but she caught herself pretty quickly. "Well, that's great. You're lucky to have so many friends."

Tomorrow, first thing, I'll call Megan and Kathy and invite them to Rachel's party.

AAARGH!!!

All I wanted was for Kathy and Megan to see Rachel's invitation for what it is: a sign that Rachel wants us all to be friends. What's so complicated about that? Instead, they acted like Rachel must have some hidden motive for including them. Even Kathy, who loves parties more than anything.

"I think the Miss Teen USA pageant's on that night," she said.

"Kathy. The Miss Teen USA pageant?"

"It's going to be really good. I saw a preview."

"Then get your mom to tape it for you."

"But then it will have already happened. The winner will already have been announced, and my opinion won't even matter."

"Kathy . . ." I tried another tactic. "Come on. Think of all the cute guys you can talk to."

"Is Jared invited?" she asked.

"Um—"

"Then why should I care? Huh? Not that you've noticed, but Jared and I are serious about each other."

"I know you are. I didn't mean—"

"I'm a one-man woman, Alli. Unlike you, I actually believe in the concept of loyalty."

I couldn't believe her. "Kathy, I'm inviting you to a *party*. I called you up to invite you to a party."

Kathy kind of *hmmph*-ed.

"So will you come?" I said. "Please?"

Kathy waited a minute, then said, "Oh, all right. *If* Megan says she'll go, and *if* I can find something to wear that doesn't make me look fat. But you better hang out with us, Alli, and not ditch us like you've been doing for the last month."

I wanted to say something back, but I held my tongue. "That's why I'm inviting you, so we can actually spend some time together. And anyway, I figured we'd all go together—you, me, and Megan." Then I remembered my promise to Rachel and winced. "I mean, unless I have to go over early to help set up."

"Uh-huh," Kathy said in a not very generous way.

"So, I'll see you Monday, okay?"

"Are you going to sit with us at lunch?" she demanded.

"Yes, I'll sit with you at lunch. I'll even open your milk for you. And now I've got to call Megan, so good-bye!"

I pressed the hang-up button, then released it and dialed Megan's number.

"Megan? Hi, it's me. Alli."

"Oh," she said. "Hey."

I could hear a little bit of weirdness in her voice, and I felt guilty for not talking to her at the History Fair.

"So, what's up?" I said. "Have you heard anything from your dad?"

"Not a word."

"Oh, Megan. That sucks."

"I know. What kind of a loser am I if my own dad won't even call?"

"*He's* the loser. Because he could be spending time with you and he's not."

"Yeah, whatever. But thanks for not clucking over me and going into the whole 'poor Megan' routine. I feel as if all anyone does these days is feel sorry for me."

"Like who?"

"Like my mom. Like Kathy, who thinks that not having a dad makes me an orphan or something. Whenever we talk about it, I get the feeling she expects me to cry." She paused. "Sometimes I even think people at school are looking at me funny, but I know I'm just being paranoid. Pathetic, huh?"

My heart stopped. I'd forgotten, in all the preparty dizziness, that maybe throwing Megan together with Rachel and the others wasn't the best idea.

"You're not pathetic," I said. *Crap*, I was thinking. *Crap, crap, crap*.

She snorted. "So what's up with you? Anything exciting going on?"

But none of them would say anything to Megan about her dad. Of course they wouldn't.

"I, uh, wanted to invite you to Rachel's birthday party," I said.

"Ex*cuse* me?" she said.

"It's this coming Friday, and Rachel asked me to invite you. Kathy, too. Kathy already said yes." I perked up my voice. "It's going to be great!"

"Rachel invited me to her party? *Why?*"

"Because she wanted to. What do you mean, why?"

"Oh my God. You didn't tell her to, did you?"

"Megan! No, I didn't *tell* her to."

"Uh-huh."

The same frustration I felt with Kathy started to nudge in with Megan. "Come on. It's going to be fun."

Megan sighed. Then she said, "Look, Alli, nothing against you, but I don't like Rachel. I don't understand what you see in her at all."

I blushed, which was totally unfair. "Megan, you've never even talked to her."

"I don't have to. I've seen the way she treats people, and it isn't nice."

"*Usually* she's nice," I said. "Usually she's *very* nice. Anyway, I don't see Kathy winning any niceness awards, and you're perfectly willing to be friends with her."

"That's different," Megan said.

"How?" I asked. I thought this was an excellent point, despite my racing heart. How *are* Rachel and Kathy all that different? If I wanted to, I could argue that Rachel is actually *better* than Kathy. Rachel only puts people down when they bug her. But Kathy puts people down—puts *me* down—in normal, ordinary life. Kathy does it to make herself look better in comparison, that's my guess. But Rachel already knows she's perfect. She has oodles of self-confidence, so in general she's happy to—what was it that Mika said? Spread the wealth.

Megan was silent. I didn't know if she was thinking about what I said or not. Part of me wanted her to respond, but part of me didn't, in case she came back with something like, "Anyway, I'm only friends with Kathy because you're never around anymore." Which, despite all the great arguments I'd made in my head, was a whole nother wad of stickiness.

Finally Megan said, "Why is it so important that I come? Why does it even matter?"

"Because I want you to. Because I want us to all get along."

I heard her breathing.

"Please?" I said.

"Rachel honestly said she wants me to come? She said that specifically?"

"*Yes.* She's inviting lots of people, and not just who'd you think. Like Jeremy Webster. He'll be there." I didn't know why I said that, especially since I knew Rachel had been kidding.

"You're comparing me to Jeremy Webster?" Megan said.

"Huh? No!"

"Then why'd you mention him?"

Good question. I wished I could go back and un-mention him.

Megan blew out a puff of air. "I have a hard time even believing that, actually," she said. "I have a hard time believing that Rachel would invite Jeremy Webster to her birthday party."

"Well, she did." *What was I saying?* "She doesn't care about stuff like who's popular and who's not."

"I'll bet," Megan said.

Her tone made me mad. She was so sure of herself, as if only she could see the truth of things. Suddenly I didn't care if she came or not.

"If you don't want to go to Rachel's party, then don't," I said. "But you're not even giving Rachel a chance. Just because someone seems a certain way on the outside doesn't mean they're that same way on the inside."

"If you say so."

"Whatever. I've got to go." And I hung up the phone.

That was twenty-seven minutes ago. I know because I've been watching the minutes change on my radio alarm.

She hasn't called back—not that I thought she would.

Same day, 11:33 A.M.

She called back. She called back!!! Here's what she said:

Megan: "Hi, Alli. It's Megan. I'm sorry for being such a jerk."

Me, not knowing how to respond: "Oh. Well . . ."

Megan: "Anyway, yeah, I'll go to Rachel's party."

Me: "You will?"

Megan: "I just get insecure sometimes, and I say stupid things. I don't know what my problem is."

Me: "Whatever. Don't worry about it."

Megan: "So, um . . ."

Me, practically bubbling over with gladness: "I'm so glad you're coming, Megan. It's going to be so much fun."

Megan, sounding not nearly so sure: "I hope so."

Me: "It will, Megan. I swear."

Monday, October 9, pre-algebra

Word of Rachel's party has spread, and kids are treating me differently because they know I'm one of the chosen. Like just now, while Mr. Schuler was putting a problem on the board, Liz Clarkson leaned over and told me she liked my watch. It's my normal old Eeyore watch, but she's never commented on it before. (It *is* pretty cute. Eeyore stares out with his big eyes, and if you push a button, he says, "Thanks for noticing me.")

And earlier, in social studies, Tory-of-the-Teddy-Bear sidled up to my desk and sucked on a strand of her hair. She drew her hair out of her mouth and said, "You're so lucky."

"I am?" I said.

She glanced at the door, where Rachel and Mika were entering with linked arms. Rachel said something to Mika, and Mika giggled.

"How did you do it?" Tory asked. "How did you make them like you?"

I didn't say anything. What *could* I say?

Then Rachel bounded over, saying, "Alli-cat! What's up?" She dropped into the seat beside me, and Tory scurried off.

Even Kathy is treating me more nicely now that it's settled that she and Megan are coming to the party. At lunch, she actually asked my opinion on what she should wear. It felt good, as if she was realizing there was more to me than she'd thought.

Ooo—close call. Mr. Schuler just asked me to tell him what x equaled if y was negative four, and of course I had no clue. I flipped through my notes, because Mr. Schuler can be mean if he thinks you're not paying attention. But right as he was heading down the aisle to whack me with his ruler or something, Carter Hunt whispered, "Thirty-seven."

"Thirty-seven," I squeaked.

Mr. Schuler stopped short. "Very good," he said.

And then Carter grinned at me. He *grinned* at me, when in

my previous existence, the most he'd ever done was step on my toe at the water fountain.

Which makes it official: I have entered a whole new land.

Tuesday, October 10, 8:10 P.M.

My nostril has healed up, the one that got all red before Rachel's slumber party. But the rest of my nose still has that clogged-pore thing going on. The question is, Should I do something about it?

There's a line from a poem Dad always quotes that goes, "Do I dare to eat a peach?" It has to do with living life to the fullest, without wimping out just because you're scared. Although why a peach would be scary is a mystery. But for me the line should be, "Do I dare to use another nose strip?"

Hmm . . .

Same night, 8:16 P.M.

Only a fool would use another nose strip after my traumatic experience.

Better safe than sorry, clogged pores and all.

Wednesday, October 11, social studies

Jeremy Webster shaved his eyebrows off.

It is unbelievable.

Apparently Rachel dared him to yesterday—I missed that part, because she did it when I wasn't around—and he said sure, if she brought him a razor. So today she winked and slipped him a pink disposable razor, which is SO against the rules.

"You really want me to do it?" Jeremy asked. "Because I will. You know I will."

"It'll be hilarious," Rachel said. "Right, girls?"

Hadley and Mika nodded (even though they were laughing as if they knew he never would), and after a second, I nodded, too. I didn't want to, but I didn't want to look like a baby.

"Go for it," I said.

So in the middle of class Jeremy asked Mr. Shakley for a bathroom pass, and when he came back, it was without his eyebrows.

The class lost it. At first Mr. Shakley was confused, and then he turned around and saw Jeremy hamming it up and blowing kisses. He marched across the room and grabbed Jeremy's arm.

"Get to the office this minute," he barked. He pulled him toward the door, but Jeremy twisted free.

"Hey!" he cried. "You can't touch me! Keep your hands off me!"

Mr. Shakley picked up the phone by the chalkboard. "Ms. Lewis? This is Mr. Shakley. I need you to send down—"

"Geez!" Jeremy said. "I'm going, okay? You don't have to call the National Guard."

Mr. Shakley glowered. "Never mind," he said into the phone. "But expect Jeremy Webster in your office in thirty seconds." He hung up, patrolling Jeremy's progress. "Come on, Webster. Move it."

"Come on, Webster, move it," Jeremy mimicked. He grinned at Rachel. Finally, he made it through the door, and Mr. Shakley exhaled.

"All right," he said. "We have ten minutes left in class. Take out a piece of paper and write a one-paragraph response to the end-of-the-chapter questions. *Now,* please."

Oh God. Mika just nudged me, then nodded toward the door. Jeremy is back, wiggling his butt in the doorway. He's barely out of Mr. Shakley's line of vision. He just turned and waggled his nonexistent eyebrows, and Mika stifled a giggle.

I don't know. I realize Rachel's doing it for me, this whole get-back-at-Jeremy thing, but I kind of wish she'd just let it go.

Same day, study hall

It's amazing how important eyebrows are. They're just these little strips of hair, but without them a person's whole face looks wrong. The forehead looks too wide, and the eyes seem too close together.

Well, one thing I know for sure. I am never shaving off my eyebrows, not for a million dollars.

Same day, 5:30 P.M.

I can't stop thinking about Jeremy's eyebrows. I wish I hadn't said, "Go for it," because that was really dumb. It made me think of this time in fourth grade when I was briefly friends with a girl named Anne Grayson. One day on the playground she said to me, "Whatever you do, don't give your swing to Tracy." No one was supposed to give her swing to Tracy. Tracy got more and more flustered, and she kept saying, "Come on, you guys. It's not fair!" Later I felt bad, even though I'd told myself at the time that I really did want to swing and that was why I wasn't getting off.

Kind of like with Jeremy. The whole mood with Rachel was daring and crazy, but the feeling in my heart was something different.

Aargh. I don't know why I'm even worrying about it. Jeremy doesn't even realize that Rachel is messing with him. In the lunch line—in front of Carter Hunt and Tad Grier and everything—Rachel saw Jeremy and called out, "Looking good!" Jeremy's ears turned pink, that's how proud he was.

Thursday, October 12, 3:45 P.M.

Today was one of those Indian summer days where the sun feels caramel warm on your skin and everyone gets a little giddy, wishing it really was summer again. In study hall we begged Ms. Chadwick to let us do our work outside. She wavered at first, saying it was against school policy and blah, blah, blah, but we wore her down by saying things like, "Oh, *please*. None of the other teachers will let us—we wouldn't even *ask* them—but you're so much cooler than they are. *Please*, Celia?"

Only now I wish we'd stayed inside, because of what happened when we got to the courtyard. Everybody found their own spot, and we honestly were doing our work (well, mainly, anyway), when I saw a bird feather on the ground beside me. I picked it up and realized it wasn't just one feather, it was a whole clump of feathers all stuck together. I looked again at the ground and saw that the grass was matted down in a strange way. Something in my head said, *Stop, you don't want to know,* but it was too late. My fingers had already pulled the grass away, and underneath was a tiny skull, or what was left of a skull. Its beak was crushed, and there were two holes where the eye sockets were.

I jerked my hand away, feeling light-headed. I grabbed my backpack and moved to a picnic table, half hoping someone would ask me what was wrong. But no one did. Ms. Chadwick was sunning herself on a concrete bench and didn't even notice.

After study hall ended, the first person I ran into was Hadley. I told her about the bird, which was a mistake. "Ew, sick!" she said, screwing up her face.

I don't know what I wanted her to say, but that wasn't it.

Same night, 8:15 P.M.

I told Mom about the dead bird, and she was much nicer about it than Hadley. We were out shopping for Rachel's birthday present, and we'd stopped for ice cream at Häagen-Dazs. I told Mom about the bird's tiny crushed beak, and she said, "Oh, sweetie." She didn't try to tell me the bird was in bird heaven or anything like that. She just said, "The world can be hard sometimes, can't it?"

But then she started asking questions about Rachel—how did we get to be such good friends, what classes did we have together?—and I completely pulled away. It's weird how one minute we'll be getting along great, and then the next minute there's, like, this wall between us.

Although I don't know if she even notices it. Maybe it's only me?

But there are some things I don't want to share with her, because when I share them, they're no longer mine.

Same night, 8:30 P.M.

Oh—I ended up getting Rachel a pair of gold earrings with tiny jade drops hanging down. They were really expensive, but they're totally worth it.

Friday, October 13, social studies

Mr. Shakley's making us do time lines, which are soooo boring. But I'm having fun anyway, because Mika and Hadley keep sneaking me looks like, "Do you think she's going to like it? Do you?" The looks have to do with Rachel's birthday cake, which we're giving her at lunch.

Mika and I already decorated her locker with streamers, balloons, and a poster that said HAPPY BIRTHDAY, RACHEL! in sparkly bubble letters. We did it during homeroom, and even Megan stopped by and said it looked cute.

"Really?" I said to her. "You like it?"

"Yeah," she said. "The green and purple streamers look cool together."

"Can you think of anything else it needs?" Mika asked.

Megan shook her head. "Seriously, it looks great." She stood there a minute, then said, "Well, see you." She shot me a quick smile and took off down the hall.

By the time we got to Mr. Shakley's room, Rachel and Hadley were already seated. Rachel was wearing a cropped sea-green sweater that showed off her belly button ring (I guess she changed into it after she left her house) and jeans that were faded but not too faded. Her hair was in a loose ponytail, and she wore tiny silver hoops in her ears. She must have taken extra care to look good since she knew she'd be getting lots of attention. And she was right: At lunch, when we give her the cake, we're going to get the whole cafeteria to sing to her.

"Rachel!" Mika said, hurrying over and giving her a hug. "Happy birthday!"

"Yeah," I said. "Happy birthday."

"Thanks, you guys. But it's no big deal." She looked around, pleased, as the other kids in the class glanced our way.

"It is so a big deal," Hadley said. "You're thirteen now. You've finally entered the teendom."

"Oh," Rachel said, "the *teendom*. That's right." She sat up and nodded to the door. "Hey. Here he comes."

Jeremy swaggered into the room without his eyebrows. Hadley whistled, and Rachel grinned and called, "Wh-hoo! Go, Jeremy!"

Jeremy made muscleman poses like he was performing for a competition, and with every new move he wiggled his nonexistent eyebrows. Everyone laughed and egged him on, including Aaron Sarmiento, who caught my eye and grinned. Earlier he'd told Rachel her party sounded fun and that he'd plan on making an appearance.

Jeremy struck one last pose, bending his knee and flexing his biceps, and then he flicked his bangs off his forehead and strutted to the back of the class.

"You are *so* hot," Rachel said as he passed her desk, and his neck turned red.

Oh my God. I just realized something incredible, only I guess it's not incredible at all.

Back when Jeremy was teasing me about the whole underwear fiasco, Kathy had gotten snickery and said he had a crush on me. And Rachel has kind of made some comments like that, too, like isn't it funny that he thinks he has a chance with me. She says that's why he shaved off his eyebrows, to impress me.

But Jeremy doesn't have a crush on me. He has a crush on Rachel.

Why didn't I see it before?

Same day, study hall

Oh, crap. Oh crap, oh crap, oh crap. Everything is messed up, and I don't know how to fix it.

It started after fourth period, when Rachel first saw her locker.

"Y'all are so sweet!" she squealed. "When did you have time to do this?" Other girls, girls who weren't coming to Rachel's party, stared at the decorated locker. Last year I would have been one of them, sneaking a quick peek at the balloons and streamers before dropping my eyes and hurrying away.

Mika smiled. "Alli and I did it before first period. Do you like it?"

"You know I do. Thanks, you guys."

"I was supposed to help, too," Hadley interrupted, "but Mr. Shakley made me meet with him about my grade. He says I have to write an extra paper, because it's obvious Tory did all the work on our stupid project. Which is completely unfair."

"And I love the sign," Rachel said, fingering the glitter paint.

"And you put little birthday cake stickers on it! It's adorable!"

"Well, come on," Mika said, sharing a look with me and Hadley. "Put your books up and let's go to lunch. I'm starved."

"Ohhh," Hadley said, doing some eye signals to show she remembered. "Right. Only I'll meet you there, okay? I've got to stop by the bathroom."

We waited while Rachel shoved her books into her locker, and she, Mika, and I headed for the cafeteria.

"My mom's having Mrs. Carlson, our housekeeper, make miniature pizzas for the party tomorrow night," Rachel said. "They're awesome. And you're bringing cookies, right, Alli?"

"Brownies," I said.

"And we'll have punch made out of orange juice and ginger ale, along with all the normal soft drinks, of course. I just think having punch makes it more sophisticated. And we bought, like, ten pounds of M&M's."

We reached the lunchroom and got in line, and Rachel described how the basement was going to be decorated, with strands of star lights from Pier 1 hanging from the ceiling and a table set up in the corner for all the presents. The girls ahead of us were eavesdropping, I could tell.

We got our spaghetti and sat down at a table near the door.

"The only thing is, I can't decide whether to wear jeans or my black dress," Rachel said, twirling her noodles on her fork. "Because jeans are more comfortable, but—"

Mika kicked me under the table. She jerked her head at the stream of people entering the cafeteria, and I saw Hadley coming toward us with a chocolate cake held carefully in front of her. The candles were lit. Not one of them had blown out.

"Ready?" Mika mouthed.

I nodded.

"So what do you think?" Rachel finished. "Jeans or the dress?"

We grinned. "Happy birthday to you, happy birthday to you!" Hadley came up behind her and put the cake in the middle of the table. "Happy *birth*day, dear Rachel, happy birthday to you!"

By the end, a bunch of other kids had joined in, and we all clapped and did drumrolls on the table.

"I can't believe it!" Rachel cried. The flames from the candles cast highlights in her hair. Her face glowed. "You got me a cake!"

"It was all of our idea," Mika said.

"But I made it," Hadley said. "And then one of the secretaries let me keep it in the office. Are you surprised?"

"Y'all are awesome," Rachel said. Her eyes shone as she looked at all the people staring our way. She blew out the candles.

She served thick slices to Hadley, Mika, and me. She put a piece on her own tray, too, the icing crumbling at the corner where the blade dug in. She tilted her head. "There's tons more," she said. "Anyone want some?"

Kids crammed around her, wishing her happy birthday while she handed out pieces of cake.

Soon there was nothing left but crumbs. At the end of the table stood Kathy and Megan, looking awkward.

"Hey, you guys," I said. I couldn't figure out why they were just standing there instead of coming over.

"Oh, no," Rachel said. "Y'all got here too late!" She considered the empty cake plate, then took her own piece and pushed it to the center of the table. "Here. You can split this one."

"Rachel!" Hadley cried.

"That's okay," Megan said.

"We just wanted to wish you happy birthday," Kathy said. She stuck her hands behind her back.

"Thanks," Rachel said. "You two *are* coming tonight, right?"

Kathy nodded, and Rachel shifted her gaze to Megan.

"Sure, I guess," Megan said.

Rachel laughed. "You *guess?* You don't sound very excited."

"No, I'm fine with it," Megan said.

Rachel tilted her head. "You're *fine* with it?"

Megan looked at her strangely. Then she looked at me, like, like, *What's with her?* "What, you want me to bow down and kiss your feet?"

My cake stuck in my throat. This was not how Megan acted. This was not how Rachel acted. *Stop it,* I silently begged them.

"Well, sorry for including you," Rachel said. "Sorry for reaching out and doing something nice."

Megan blushed. "I didn't mean it like that."

"No, really. Obviously you'd rather sit at home and mope than come to my party."

"I just meant—"

"But listen, sweetie. Just because your dad up and left doesn't mean you can take it out on me."

For a second, no one got what she'd said. I sure didn't. Then her words sank in, and my insides twisted.

"Wh-what?" Megan said.

Rachel scooped up a dab of icing. She popped it in her mouth.

Megan turned to me. *"Alli?!"*

I could hardly breathe. "Megan . . ."

"You promised you wouldn't tell," she said, blinking back tears. "You promised!" She turned and ran from the table.

"Megan!" I cried.

"You suck, Alli," Kathy said. She hurried after Megan.

I watched them go. I felt as if I were separating from my body.

"You suck, Alli," Hadley mimicked, squenching her words.

"Hadley, don't," Mika said in a low voice.

I turned to Rachel. I saw worry flick across her face.

"Who needs them, anyway?" she said.

"Talk about rude," Hadley said.

I didn't say a word.

Same day, still in study hall

Ms. Chadwick just dropped her cup of coffee, and it splattered all over her white blouse. "Damn," she wailed. "I just bought this yesterday!"

The class hushed. Then Mary Ann Singleton used a spooky voice to say, "Oooo, it's because it's Friday the thirteenth. Everything always goes wrong on Friday the thirteenth!"

I wish I'd never been born.

Just got an e-mail from Kathy. Here's what it said:

> Are you happy now that you've ruined Megan's life?
> You think just because Rachel likes you, all of a sudden
> you're special. You don't even realize what you're turning
> into, do you? But everyone can see right through you.

My body got hot when I read it, and I punched DELETE.
I also got an e-mail from Rachel herself. Here's what *it* said:

> *Oh my God, Alli, I am so sorry about what happened at lunch*
> *today. I shouldn't have said that about Megan's dad. I don't even*
> *know why I did.*
> *I hope you can forgive me, at least for tonight.*
> *Hugs and kisses,*
> *Rachel*
> *P.S. Megan DID piss me off, the way she was acting like she was*
> *doing me this huge honor by coming to the party. But she's your*
> *friend, so I should have let it go.*

I don't know what I think, other than if someone knows she
shouldn't say something, then she shouldn't say it, plain and
simple. Like what Rachel said about Hadley being oversexed,
that night at her slumber party. It's not fair to say something
and then take it back.

Crap. Mom's done cutting the brownies, and she's calling me
from the kitchen. She's ready to drive me to the party.

Later, in Rachel's basement

I feel like I'm both here and not here. Like I'm buried deep inside my body, and maybe I look the same on the outside, but on the inside I'm just a fleck.

Supposedly, I'm sorting CDs. Supposedly I'm making a song list so that the party will have a theme. So far I've picked out two depressing-looking Nirvana CDs and one other by Sheryl Crow. But I haven't put them on.

This is so weird, sitting here by myself while the party spins on without me. It's like last year all over again, when I came back to school and no longer knew anything. It's like I don't even know how to be me.

Mika just came over, and I had to shove this notebook behind the rack of CDs. Now that she's gone, I've pulled it out again. (Obviously.) I didn't bring my real journal—too risky—but I saw this little spiral in the side pocket of Mom's car and shoved it into my mini-backpack. I'll paste these pages in when I get home, I guess. It helps to be writing this all out. It makes me feel a teeny bit connected to the real me, although not enough.

Anyway, Mika asked if something was the matter, and I almost told her. After all, she didn't laugh when Rachel was such a jerk in the cafeteria. Although she didn't stand up to her, either.

"Is it because Aaron Sarmiento isn't here?" Mika said. "Because he's coming. I know he is."

"Yeah, I know."

"Then what's wrong?"

I looked at her. She held my gaze for maybe a second.

"Well, come find me when you're done sorting the CDs," she said. Then she left, which is why I'm busy writing again.

Oh my God. Forget Mika, and forget the dumb CDs.

Jeremy Webster just walked down the stairs. JEREMY WEBSTER. He's wearing black jeans and a white button-down I didn't even know he owned, and with his hair combed back I almost didn't recognize him. But it's him, all right. His eyebrows are just barely starting to grow back.

Why is he here? Did Rachel actually invite him, for real?

Carter and Tyler slapped Jeremy's hand when they saw him, but now they're smirking. The girls are all drawing back as he passes.

He's heading for Rachel. He's holding a box wrapped in silver paper. Rachel doesn't notice him—she's chatting with some eighth grader—and my stomach is tensing. This feels wrong, wrong, wrong.

He's there. She's turning her head. Jeremy is nervous, I can see it by how he's gripping his present, but Rachel smiles when she sees him, saying, "Jeremy! You came!" So why do I feel so worried?

Now Rachel's doing some weird flirty thing that she would never do with Jeremy in real life. She's cocking her head and touching Jeremy's collar, telling him how *sweet* he is to bring her a present, and Jeremy is gulping and trying to act cool. The kids standing near them are laughing, although some are trying to hide it. Why is Jeremy not catching on?

Rachel just stepped closer, pressing her body against his. Jeremy has gone totally rigid. Rachel's saying, "But what I *really* want is a kiss. Aren't you going to give me a birthday kiss? Just one eensy-weensy kiss?"

But Jeremy *has* to see through her. How can he possibly think she's serious, even with her fingers now tracing the line of his jaw?

Oh no. Why is Jeremy wetting his lips? Why is he leaning toward her?

NO!!!! DON'T DO IT, JEREMY!!!!

I can't bear to watch.

Same night, the sidewalk in front of Kwik-Mart

Mom and Dad are going to kill me. I could hear it in their voices when I called them.

"What were you thinking?" Dad said when I told him where I was. "Why in the world didn't you call us from Rachel's house, instead of a Kwik-Mart half a mile away?"

I pressed the phone against my ear.

Mom got on and said, "Allison, it really worries me that you would walk by yourself to a gas station, when we've told you a thousand times how dangerous it is to be on the streets by yourself!"

"It's only eight-fifteen," I said. "And it's not like Rachel's neighborhood is the murder capital of the world."

"Don't fool yourself," Mom said. "Bad things happen everywhere."

I scrunched lower in the phone booth. *She* was telling *me* this?

After Jeremy kissed Rachel—and I *did* watch, I couldn't help it—all hell had broken loose. It wasn't even a real kiss, although it *was* lip to lip. It was more of a peck. Still, Rachel totally flipped out.

"Ew," she had said, wiping her mouth. *"Ewww!"*

Hadley sprinted over. She looked from Rachel to Jeremy and back again. "Oh my God, you are in so much trouble," she said to Jeremy.

"Huh?" Jeremy said.

Hadley put her arm around Rachel, who said, "I'm sorry, Hadley, but I just can't handle this. Oh God—he kissed me!"

The eighth grader Rachel had been chatting with glared at Jeremy. "You're sick, man."

Carter and Tyler joined the eighth grader and crossed their arms across their chests.

Jeremy clutched his present. "But she said . . . and she was—"

"You actually thought I was *serious?*" Rachel cried.

"You're such a waste," the eighth grader said.

Jeremy searched the room. His eyes found mine, and shame curled in my stomach. The entire room was silent except for the Staind CD I'd put on ten minutes earlier.

Finally Jeremy broke the spell. A deep shade of red crept up his neck, past his Adam's apple, and over his whole face. He flung the present at Rachel's feet. "You think I want to be at this stupid party?" he said. He strode forward and swept his arm across the refreshment table. Brownies flew through the air along with Mom's plate, which landed on the carpet and bounced.

Hadley shrieked.

"Screw you," Jeremy said. "Screw all of you!" He ran upstairs and out of the basement, slamming the door behind him.

For a moment, no one knew how to react. Then Carter stuck out his chin and said, "Nice try, Webster," even though Jeremy was no longer there to hear.

"I can't believe he *kissed* you," an eighth-grade girl said to Rachel. "Omigod, you could totally sue. Or not *sue*, but . . . you know. Ream him for sexual harassment."

Another girl bit at her thumbnail. "Does he *like* you? As in *like* you like you?"

Rachel gave a shaky laugh. "Don't be disgusting."

I stood up. I walked to the stairs.

Mika broke free from the crowd. "Alli?" she said.

"I'm leaving," I said.

"Why?"

I looked at her like, *You're kidding, right?*

"Because of Jeremy?" she asked.

"Uh, yeah," I said. "Rachel publicly humiliated him, if you didn't notice."

"I know. But come on, he kind of deserved it."

My fingers squeezed into fists. He did *not* deserve it. *Nobody* deserved to be treated like that.

"Anyway, you're not really one to judge," she went on. "She did it for you."

"For *me?* What do I have to do with it?"

Mika glanced at Hadley, who had begun cleaning up the mess. Behind her, some of the others had started dancing again.

"Don't play dumb," Mika said. "All that Pussycat Palace stuff?" She gestured impatiently. "Rachel was paying him back."

My throat closed.

"If you didn't like it, you should have said something," she said. "It's not like you didn't know."

There was a fuzziness in my brain, and I didn't want to think about what she was telling me. Only I couldn't help it, because there it was in front of us, out in the open for everyone to see.

I looked past Mika at Rachel, who was watching us but pretending not to. Our eyes met, and she quickly switched her gaze to Carter Hunt. She touched his arm and laughed at what he was saying.

I took a breath. I started toward her.

"Alli, what are you doing?" Mika said. *"Alli?"*

Rachel was wearing the same strappy black heels she'd had on when I saw her at that chichi restaurant, and her black dress hung just right on her body. She made herself very animated as she talked to Carter.

I came up behind her. "You can't treat people like that," I said.

She turned. She welcomed me with a smile, as if she just that second realized I was there. "Alli! Having fun?"

"It isn't right." My heart thumped, because saying it took courage I didn't really have.

"I'm sorry, what?"

"You know what I'm talking about."

Carter must have felt something pass between us, because he held up his hands. "Chill, babe. It's just a party." As he backed away, he said to Tyler, "Watch out, man. Catfight."

Rachel's smile tightened. She waited until Carter was out of earshot, then said, "Is this about Jeremy? Because you're pretty much picking the wrong time."

I tried to keep it together. It *was* about Jeremy, but it was about more than that, too.

"You can't just do whatever you want whenever you feel like it," I said. I hated the way my voice sounded, all stupid and trembly. "Like yesterday. You shouldn't have said that stuff about Megan."

"*Ohhh,*" Rachel said. She gave me a knowing look to suggest that now she understood what all the fuss was about. "Don't worry about Megan. She's just jealous."

I faltered. "Of what?"

She poked me in the ribs. "Of you, goof."

"*Why?*"

Rachel scanned the room, full of people who wanted to be near her. She trained her gaze back on me, for the moment the nearest of them all. "Alli-cat. Get real."

I closed my eyes. She was reminding me of how lucky I was, and I was suddenly afraid she was right. How messed up is that? But then I remembered Megan's expression in the cafeteria. It made a sick spot inside of me.

When I opened my eyes, Rachel was still there. For a flickering second she seemed uncertain.

"I'm not a bad person," she said.

"What you did was wrong," I said. "It was, Rachel."

Her face hardened. "Fine," she said.

Hadley materialized at her side. "What's going on?" she asked. "Is everything okay?"

Rachel ignored her. To me, she said, "You're welcome, you know. For carrying you all this way." She arched her eyebrows. "But I think you're done now."

My head buzzed. Everyone was staring.

"I think so, too," I said.

I was afraid I wouldn't be able to make my legs work. But I did. I walked upstairs and out the front door, and I kept walking until I got here, where I called Mom and Dad. The Kwik-Mart guy keeps peering out the door at me, and I wish they'd hurry up and arrive.

I want to go home.

Same night, 10:59 P.M.

Well, I'm not grounded, but only because Mom and Dad feel sorry for me. They know something happened at the party, even though I told them I don't want to talk about it. So they're not punishing me, but I'm supposed to think about what I did. Like there's any way I could avoid it.

It's all Rachel's fault. Everything. I can't believe I stood up for her all those times when Kathy and Megan tried to tell me what she was like. I can't believe I was so dumb.

I keep seeing Jeremy's face when that eighth grader shoved him in the chest. I keep seeing his present on the floor, its paper torn at one corner. I wonder if Rachel opened it. She probably did, then held it up so everyone could laugh.

Oh no. I left my present, too, sitting on the table with the others. I wonder if she liked it. I can't believe I care.

Same night, 11:25 P.M.

God. I just realized something terrible. I stood up for Rachel, but I didn't stand up for Jeremy. At least, not in time to make a difference. And I didn't stand up for Megan in time to make a difference, either. Because I am a horrible, awful person.

Saturday, October 14, 11:00 A.M.
Life sucks.

Same day, 1:01 P.M.
I suck.

Same day, 2:12 P.M.
I'm going back to bed.

Same day, 4:45 P.M.
Kathy just called. Mom had to wake me up to answer the phone, and when she came into my room, she was all, "Alli? Why are you asleep in the middle of the afternoon?" She gave me a concerned look. "Do you want to talk, sweetie?"

But I couldn't even if I'd wanted to, because I had to take the phone and talk to Kathy, although *talk* isn't really the word. She was so mean. It was as if the fact that I'd told Rachel about Megan made me officially evil, which in Kathy's mind meant that she no longer had to even pretend to be nice. She could treat me however she wanted.

"So how was the party?" she asked. "Was it so *wonderful*? Was it so *amazing*?"

"Kathy . . ." I said.

"I just hope it was worth it, that's all. I hope it was worth it to sell out your friends. Did you spill any more secrets while you were there? Huh?"

"Actually, I—"

"You're so desperate for approval, it's ridiculous. I wouldn't be you for a million dollars."

"Kathy, you're not even—"

"They don't really like you, you know. They don't even know you. *I'm* the one who was there when you porked out last year. *I'm* the one who stuck around when you were all, 'Oh poor me, I have no friends, boo hoo hoo.' Because I felt sorry for you, in case you were wondering. Because you're pathetic. My God, you came to school with a pair of *underwear* hanging out of your pants. Do you honestly think you're Rachel material?"

"*Stop,*" I said. I clenched the phone. "I don't *want* to be Rachel material. I don't want to be anything. And you can stop beating me up, because believe it or not, I'm doing a good enough job myself, all right?" I swallowed hard. I was *not* going to cry. "So *leave me alone.*"

Kathy was stunned into silence.

"Good-bye, Kathy," I said. I hung up the phone.

Sunday, October 15, 9:15 A.M.

The person I really want to talk to is Megan.

But I'm scared.

Same day, 9:48 A.M.

I'm not going to call her, because she'll just hang up on me. I want to go see her in person. But what will I say?

I think Mom will take me, if I ask. I just went downstairs to get something to drink, and she and Dad were sitting at the table sipping their coffee.

"Hey there, sleepyhead," Mom said. "How are you doing this morning?"

"Terrible," I said. I lingered in the doorway. "I'm a terrible person."

"Allison," she chided. She gestured to the chair beside her, and reluctantly I came over. "Are you going to tell us about it?"

"There's nothing to tell. I'm a jerk. I told someone something about someone, and that person is never going to forgive me."

"Ohhh," Dad said. Then, to Mom, "Did you get any of that?"

"Dan, hush," Mom said. "Fix Alli something to eat."

"I'm not hungry," I said.

Dad lumbered up from the table. He poured me some juice and set it in front of me.

"Have you told whoever it is that you're sorry?" Mom asked.

"There's no point. She won't believe me."

"Have you tried?"

I swirled my juice. It turned out I wasn't so thirsty after all.

"You have to try, Alli," Mom said. She smoothed my hair, and a lump rose in my throat. "I know it's hard. But there's kind of no way around it."

"But what if she won't listen?" I said.

Dad jumped in—he always has to solve the world's problems—and said that in that case, I'd have to make a "grand gesture" to show I really meant it. "Like when Romeo stabbed himself in the heart to prove his love for Juliet," he said in his teacher's voice.

"Well, there's no need to be that dramatic," Mom said.

Only I think maybe he's right, although not with a dagger, obviously. I've got to come up with the perfect grand gesture to show Megan I'm sorry. Because I think I've been wrong in the way I thought about friends. And if Megan doesn't forgive me, I'll die.

Same day, 10:31 A.M.

Oh my God. I just figured it out—of course!

Same day, Lenox Mall

Grown-ups—aargh! First Mom had to talk to the pet store lady, and now she's on her cell with Megan's mother, checking it out with her. I think Mom was surprised that it was Megan I was worried about, not Kathy, but I was like, "Yeah, Mom. Megan. Could we hurry it up, please?"

I didn't want to explain what I'd figured out, which is that Kathy really is much more like Rachel than she'll ever know. They're like evil twins—one who's popular and one who's not—and turns out I'm not interested in being friends with *either* of them. Friends are supposed to make you feel good about yourself, not bad. Anyway, just because Kathy and I were friends last year doesn't mean we have to be friends forever.

Megan, on the other hand . . .

I really, really, really want to make things right.

Same day, Megan's house

Hurray!!!

I can breathe again.

Megan's hunting down a bigger box to make a bed in, and I'm sitting here on Megan's beanbag chair while Fred Junior tackles my toes.

Fred Junior is Megan's new kitten. He's butterscotch colored with golden eyes, and he's adorable. On each of his paws he has six toes, which the pet store lady said was very unusual.

At first I thought Megan was going to turn us both away. Mom was watching from the car, and I had a plunging fear of how embarrassing it would be if Megan slammed the door in my face.

Instead, Megan's face got stiff, and she said, "Please tell me that's not a cat. *Please* tell me you didn't show up here with a cat."

"Just take him," I said, holding out the cardboard pet carrier. "Not because you're mad at me, and not because I think it'll make everything magically better . . ."

Megan crossed her arms in front of her chest.

I pulled back the carrier, resting one edge on my hip. "Megan, I am so sorry. I never meant to tell, I swear. It just slipped out. And then Rachel . . . she's such a jerk . . . and—" All the awful feelings from last night came flooding back, and my eyes welled up. My nose started to run, but with my arms full I couldn't even use my sleeve to wipe it. "Just take him, will you?"

From inside the carrier came a squeaky meow.

Megan let herself look. Fred Junior mewed again.

"He wants out," I said.

She pressed her lips together, then took the carrier from my hands and carried it into the house. She opened the flaps, and there he was. He stretched his mouth into a yawn.

"Hey, little guy," Megan whispered. She lifted him out. Fred Junior put his paw on her leg, and for several minutes they were in their own little world as she scratched his head. And then I ruined it by announcing, "He has six toes on each paw. Isn't that cool?"

Megan withdrew her hand. Fred Junior tried to nudge her back into action, but she didn't relent.

"Megan—"

"You can't expect things to be better, just like that."

"I know."

"You can't waltz in here and give me a *kitten*, for God's sake, and assume I'll just forgive you."

"That's not . . . I never thought that, Megan."

Fred Junior climbed onto Megan's thigh and tried to worm his way under her fingers.

"What happened at the party?" she asked. It came out mad, as if she were angry at herself for wanting to know.

I told her. I told her what Rachel did to Jeremy, and how I stood there and let it happen. When I finished, Megan gazed at me.

"And then you just left?" she asked. "Right there in the middle of the party?"

I remembered how naked I felt with everyone watching. I nodded.

"Well, looks like you're going to be on their bad list for the next thousand years." She narrowed her eyes. "Is that why you're here? You don't have your cool friends anymore, so you thought I'd be better than nothing?"

I could feel blood rush to my face. "No! You don't really think that, do you?" *You're cooler than any of them,* I wanted to say.

Megan looked down. She moved her hand toward Fred Junior, grazing his cheek but not really stroking him.

"It was worse than the first day of school," I said. Her expression told me she was listening. "I didn't feel like myself inside. I guess . . . I don't know. Maybe I haven't in a while."

Megan rubbed her finger down Fred Junior's nose. Then she scooped him up and held him close. "I love him," she said into his fur. "I'm going to call him Fred Junior. Or would that be too stupid?"

The breath in my chest started to loosen. "I don't think it would be stupid at all."

And now I have to stop writing, because Megan's back with the box. She's trying to make it nice by putting blankets inside and one of her old stuffed animals for a chew toy, but Fred Junior keeps attacking the cardboard flaps. It's kind of funny, actually—he's just so *cute*—but I have to go help before he messes everything up. It's going to take both of us to do it right.

TURN THE PAGE FOR A PREVIEW OF

Twelve

March

THE THING ABOUT BIRTHDAYS, especially if you just that very day turned twelve, is that you should make a point of trying to look good. Because twelve is almost thirteen, and thirteen is a teenager, and teenagers don't strut around with holes in their jeans and ketchup on their shirts.

Well. They did if they were my sister, Sandra, who was fifteen-about-to-turn-sixteen. Her birthday comes next month, which meant that for a delightful three-and-a-half-week period beginning today, she was only three years older than me, instead of four. *Yes!*

Sandra made a show of not caring about her appearance, although it was clear she secretly did. She stayed in the bathroom far longer than any human needed to, and I knew she was in there staring and staring and staring at herself in the mirror: putting on eyeliner and then wiping all but the barest trace of it off; dabbing on the tiniest smidge of Sun Kissed Cheek Stain from the Body Shop; making eyes at herself and dreaming about Bo, her boyfriend, who told her he liked her just the way she was—natural. So ha ha, the trick was on Bo, but I've learned from Sandra that boys were often like that: clueless, but not necessarily in a bad way. When I am fifteen, I'll probably have a boyfriend, and I'll probably be just like Sandra. I'll want to look pretty, but not like I'm trying.

But today was my birthday, not Sandra's, and I felt like pulling out all the stops. Dressing up usually felt dumb to me—I left that to snooty Gail Grayson and the other sixth-grade go-go girls—but I had a tingly special-day feeling inside. Plus, we were leaving in half an hour for my fancy birthday dinner at Benihana's. Bo was going to meet us there, and so was Dinah, my new best friend. Although it still felt weird calling her that.

I tugged my lemon yellow ballerina skirt from the clippy things on the hanger and wrapped it around my waist. I threaded one tie through the hole at the side, then swooped it around and knotted it in place. When Mom bought this skirt for me six months ago, she had to show me how to make it work, and I'd found it impossibly complicated. Not anymore.

A full-length mirror hung on the inside of my closet door, and I twirled in front of it and watched the fabric swish around my knees. I had scabs from Rollerblading and a scrape from exploring a sewage pipe, but who cared? I could be beautiful *and* tough. I refused to buff away the calluses on my feet, too. Mom said a girl's feet should be soft, but I said, "Uh, no." I was proud of my calluses. I'd worked hard for them. Summer was right around the corner, and I wasn't about to wince my way across the hot concrete when I went to the neighborhood pool. Flip-flops were for wimps. For me, it's barefoot all the way.

I rifled through my clothes until I found my black tank top. Sleek and sophisticated—yeah. People would think I was from New York instead of Atlanta. But when I wiggled into it, I realized something was wrong. It was tight—as in, *really* tight. I flexed my shoulder blades forward and then backward, trying to loosen things up. Then forward and backward again. But what I saw in the mirror was bad. With my herky-jerky shoulders, I looked like a chicken. With breasts.

"Mo-o-om!" I called. "We've got a problem!"

"What?" Mom called back.

"We've got a *problem*!" I yelled.

"Winnie, I can't hear you. If you need me, you're going to have to come here!"

I skittered down the long hall to Mom and Dad's bedroom. My skirt fluttered against my legs.

"Look," I said. Mom was in her bra and underwear, picking out her own outfit, and she was so much curvier than I was. Than I would ever be, I was pretty sure. And that was okay. I didn't want to be curvy. I didn't even want to be . . . bumpy.

Mom turned and took me in. "Winnie, you look *adorable*," she said. And then, "Oh." And then, "My goodness, Winnie. You're *developing*."

I turned bright red. I could feel it. I crossed my arms high over my chest and said, "What am I supposed to do?"

"Well, you're going to need to pick another top," she said. She put her arm around me and rubbed my bare shoulder. "And I guess we need to go bra shopping, don't we?"

"No no no no no," I said. "Let's not overreact here, all right?" Bras were for go-go girls. Bras were for Gail Grayson, who just last week made a huge stinking deal out of how cool she was because she wore one, while not everyone else in the sixth grade did. Like me and Dinah, to be specific. No way was I going to slink to school with telltale strap lines under my shirt, making Gail believe I actually cared what she thought.

"Sweetie, there's nothing wrong with wearing a bra," Mom said. "It's life. It's the way the world works. It means you're on the brink of womanhood."

"Whoa," I said. I held up my hand, palm out. "Enough, okay?"

She smiled like she thought I was being funny. But I did not want my mother telling me I was on the brink of womanhood. What next? Orthopedic shoes with squishy soles? Dentures?

"You'll probably be getting your period soon, too," Mom said.

"*Beep, beep, beep!* Alert! Alert!" I wiggled out of her grasp and backed toward the door.

"Winnie . . ."

"Got to run. See you!"

I dashed to my room and ducked into my closet, pulling the door shut behind me. I pulled off the tank top, scrunched it into a ball, and dropped it out of sight behind my Little People Castle, which I had yet to pass on to my younger brother, Ty, who was five. I allowed Ty to play with it—together we'd drop Little People through the dungeon's trapdoor and go "*Ahhh!*"—but I wasn't ready to give up possession. Even though Mom said I was too old for it. Even though Sandra said, "Sheesh, Winnie. Grow up already, will you?"

Naked except for my skirt and underwear, I confronted myself in the mirror. It was true: I was no longer flat as a pancake. I had strong arms and a smooth, firm belly and . . .

Boobs.

I was with boob. I was boobful. I was boobed.

I, Winifred Perry, had boobs.

I sank down onto the floor, scrunching my knees up in front of me. How had this happened? I didn't want this. Boobs were for other people, not me. I didn't even like the word *boobs*, although *breasts* was a thousand times worse.

Dinah had boobs, soft little humps that provoked Gail's bra attack on the playground last week. "It's really kind of embarrassing the way certain people bounce around," Gail had said, shooting a sidelong glance at Dinah. "Especially with boys nearby."

Gail's boobs were even bigger than Dinah's. She let her bra straps show on purpose. Sometimes they were purple.

Amanda, who used to be my best friend but who had dumped me for Gail, had also gone the way of the bra, although she did not have boobs.

Which was worse: to have boobs, or not to have boobs?

I didn't want to be boobless *forever*. I just wasn't sure I wanted them now. Today they were starter boobs, no bigger than cotton balls, but what if they kept growing? I thought of a poem Ty had learned at the library, which ended like this: *They grew and they grew and they never stopped, they grew and they grew till the darn things popped!*

The poem was about pea pods. But what if it was in code?

I leaned forward, still looking in the mirror, and bent my arms at the elbow. I placed my bent arms over my chest like big, pendulous breasts. They didn't look like breasts, they looked like elbows, but if I let my sight go hazy, I could create the illusion.

I was ginormous.

The doorknob clicked, and Sandra poked her head into the closet. She saw me on the floor with my elbow-boobs.

"Oh my God. What are you *doing*?" she demanded.

"Nothing!" I scrambled up and grabbed a white button-down.

"It's time to go. Dad's turning the car around."

"I'm getting ready," I said. "A little privacy, please?"

Sandra shook her head. "You just today turned twelve and already you've got attitude? Great, this is just great."

I made a big "ahem" sound.

"Well, hurry," she said. She strode away, leaving the closet door wide open.

At Benihana's, Dinah flittered with excitement. "You look fantastic," she said to me in the waiting area. "You look so *old*. I love your shirt—it looks so cute like that!"

"Thanks," I said. I'd paired a white T-shirt with a white button-down, and I'd tied the ends of the button-down at my waist. My boobs were safely hidden by the double layers, plus the knotted waist of the button-down made the fabric poof out in a way that was very concealing.

"You look nice, too," I told Dinah.

Dinah beamed. She wore a pink dress with a built-in vest. As always, she was one step off in terms of the whole fashion thing. She looked more like she was going to church than going out to dinner. She even carried a small, white leather pocketbook.

"Right this way," the hostess said. She led us to a sunken table at the back of the restaurant. "Shoes here," she said, gesturing to a mat on the floor.

Dinah watched as Dad slipped off his loafers. Mom stepped out of her clogs, and Dinah edged closer to me.

"We have to take our shoes off?" she said.

"Uh-huh," I said. "That's the way they do it in Japan."

"But . . . what if my feet stink?"

"Did you take a shower?" I asked. Dinah's mom died way back when she was a baby, and sometimes she had to be reminded of the basics.

"Yes," she said. "Yesterday I did."

"Then I'm sure your feet are fine," I said. "Anyway, they'll be under the table, not plopped on top with the Poo Poo Platter."

Dinah's eyes widened. "We're having *Poo Poo Platter*?"

"That's Chinese, not Japanese," Sandra said, using her toe to nudge her Chuck Taylors onto the mat. "Stop teasing and be nice."

"She's right," I whispered to Dinah. "We're actually having fish heads."

Sandra rapped me with her knuckles.

"*Ow*," I said.

The waiter, who had an impressive Fu Manchu mustache, chopped and diced on a steel griddle right in front of us. Oil sizzled, and Dinah shrank back. A snow pea got too hot and exploded; Dinah squealed.

"What's he doing now?" she asked as he slid an upside-down bowl onto the hissing griddle.

"Shrimp," I said. "Yummy yum yum."

The waiter lifted the bowl, and two dozen raw shrimp spilled out, sputtering in the heat. They looked as if they were dancing. I grinned at Dinah, but Dinah didn't grin back.

"Uh . . . Dinah?" I said.

She gulped. "I don't . . . I can't—"

"Do you not like shrimp? Are you allergic?"

"I'm not allergic, I just . . ." Her eyes flew to Bo, who sat on the opposite side of the table with Sandra. He was showing Ty how to bounce water up inside a straw by tapping the end with his finger.

I lowered my voice. "You just what?"

Dinah gave me a pleading look. "I'm scared of them."

A whoop burst out of me. "Of *shrimp*? You're scared of shrimp?"

"Shhh," she said. "They're so pale. And they've got . . . veins."

"Really *big* veins," I said. "Help! They're coming to get me! Attack of the veins!"

She giggled despite herself. "Don't let him give me any, okay? I mean it."

In part she was being goofy, but in part she meant it, too. She was funny that way, always wanting me to protect her—which usually I didn't mind because it made me feel important. It was something I noticed, though. My friendship with Dinah was so different from my friendship with Amanda, who'd been much more of an . . . equal.

Ooo, shove that thought back down. Dinah was an equal, too. Just a different kind of equal.

Dad clinked his fork against his glass, and I was glad for the distraction. I sat up tall and nudged Dinah to do the same.

"A toast," Dad said.

"Hear, hear!" said Ty. He loved making toasts.

"To my wonderful daughter on her twelfth birthday," Dad said.

"Oh God, here we go," said Sandra.

"May she learn the value of a tidy room and a tidy desk, and may she realize that when it comes to stuffing the toilet with gummy worms, her father does indeed know best."

"Da-a-ad," I said. I'd put gummy worms in the toilet *once*, when I was like Ty's age.

"May she always stay true to her kind and generous heart," he said. "And may she stay our little girl forever."

He gazed at me. There was love in his eyes, and it made me embarrassed, but happy, too.

"Cheers!" cried Ty, lifting his Shirley Temple. "Everybody clink!"

I clinked my glass with Dinah's, and then with Dad's. Then Mom's and Sandra's and Bo's and Ty's.

"Happy birthday, sweetie," Mom said.

"Yeah, yeah, happy birthday," said Sandra.

"Happy birthday," said the Fu Manchu waiter. He flipped a sizzling pink shrimp at me, but it missed my plate and landed on Dinah's. Or maybe that's what he intended all along. Dinah shrieked, and everyone laughed.

Ty went to bed at nine, and at ten, Mom and Dad retired to their room to watch the news. By eleven, I was pretty tired, and I think Dinah was, too, but we weren't the slightest bit ready to go to sleep. Punch-drunk, Mom would have called us. Everything I said made Dinah laugh, and everything Dinah said made me laugh. Sandra kept stomping into my room to tell us to be quiet, and each time she looked grumpier and grumpier. The last time she had a mud mask smeared over her face, and I said, "Better wipe that frown off, young lady, or it'll stick like that." Dinah about busted a gut.

After Sandra left, I said, "She puts that on to clean her pores. Isn't that weird, to use mud to clean your face?"

"She's so pretty," Dinah said. She scratched my cat, Sweetie-Pie, behind the ears, and Sweetie-Pie head-butted her in pleasure. "Is it fun having a sister who's so pretty?"

"*Ehh,*" I said. Sandra *was* pretty, but mainly she was just Sandra. "Want me to see if she'll let us use some of her mask?"

"Yeah!" Dinah said.

"It's really neat," I said, getting to my feet. "It tightens on your face until you can't smile, and it feels like you're para- lyzed. Hold on, I'll be right back."

I padded across the hall to Sandra's room, but she was on the phone with Bo. I held up my finger to mean, "Just one little thing? Real quick?" She scowled and turned her back to me.

Well, I thought to myself. *How rude.* I walked in plain sight to her bathroom and grabbed the tub of mask, then darted in pouncy, tiptoe steps back across the hall.

"Mission accomplished!" I announced. I plopped down on the floor, and Dinah scooted closer.

"So what do we do?" she asked.

I picked up Sweetie-Pie and tossed her onto the bed, because mud and fur don't mix. Then I unscrewed the lid of the container. "We smear it all over, and then we let it dry." I wiped a fingerful across my cheek. It was cool and oozy. "Now that I'm twelve, I guess I better start thinking about these things. Pores and stuff."

"How does it feel being twelve?" Dinah asked. "Does it feel different?"

I liked the way she was regarding me, as if I were the wise one because I was older.

"Hmm," I said. "Mainly it feels the same . . . but yeah, I guess it is different." I hesitated, then said, "My mom says it's time for me to get a bra."

"Really?"

I shrugged inside my oversized Braves nightshirt. "Not like tomorrow or anything. I mean, it's not *desperate*."

Dinah swiped on one last blob of mud, and a little got in her hair. "Whoops," she said.

"In fact I'm kind of hoping she'll forget about it," I said. "Because once you start wearing a bra, you can't turn back. It's like shaving your legs."

"It is?"

"Well, with legs, the hair comes back pricklier once you start shaving, so you really shouldn't start unless you're ready to commit forever and ever. Same with bras."

"Your boobs come back pricklier?" Dinah said.

I giggled. "Uh-huh. Like cactuses."

She giggled, too. "What are you *talking* about?"

"Imagine if a boy tried to touch them. '*Ooo*, baby, I'm feeling so romantic—*ouch*!'"

"Stop making me laugh!" she said. "You're making my face crack!"

"You look like the Creature from the Black Lagoon. Want to see?" I scrambled up and grabbed my hand mirror from my bureau. I very sneakily grabbed something else, too: a little souvenir from Benihana's that I'd plucked from my plate and wrapped in a paper napkin to bring home. I hadn't known what I'd do with it until now.

"Close your eyes," I said, "and don't open them till I say 'three.' Okay? One, two . . . three!"

Dinah opened her eyes. She saw the shrimp dangling in front of her nose.

"*Eeeee!*" she screamed.

I wiggled it closer. "It's coming to get you! It's coming to get you!"

"Nooo!"

Sweetie-Pie meowed in alarm.

Sandra burst into the room. "God!" she complained. "For the fifty millionth time, do you have to be so—" She stopped, noticing our cakey faces. "Did you use my mud mask? Without asking?"

I widened my eyes. In my sweetest, nicest voice, I said, "Er . . . care for a shrimp?"

Sandra took in the limp pink shrimp swaying between my fingers. Disgust layered itself over her outrage. "You are *so* immature," she said.

"*Au contraire, mon frère,*" I protested. "In case you've forgotten, I am twelve years old. I'm on the brink of womanhood."

"Could have fooled me," she retorted. She snatched the container of mask, stormed out of the room, and slammed the door.

"Sandra, Sandra, Sandra," I said, shaking my head. "Do you have to be so loud?"

Dinah collapsed in hysterics.